Chelsea was in Connor's arms again. . . .

Suddenly they were standing in front of each other by the bed. Chelsea watched as Connor's eyes focused on her, and for a brief moment she saw the longing in them, and recognized it. Before she could stop herself, she knew the same feelings showed in her own eyes. Connor was standing so close to her.

She had a sudden desire to touch him again. To feel him hold her. And then, as though she'd asked for it, she felt his arms come around her waist. The moment he touched her, there was a thrill. The same electricity she'd felt that first time last summer when he'd kissed her on the beach, and later when she'd crept into his room in the middle of the night, curious and full of longing.

She closed her eyes as Connor's face neared hers. It truly was one of her favorite images. His handsome, lovely, freckled Irish face coming toward her.

She forgot all about the work they were supposed to be doing. The fact that they weren't living together anymore. All of the fights they'd had.

All Chelsea could think of as she hit the bed was that she was happy. And she was in her husband's arms again.

Look for these other titles in the
Ocean City series:

Ocean City
Love Shack
Fireworks
Boardwalk
Ocean City Reunion
Heat Wave

And don't miss

Katherine Applegate's
romantic new series!

#1 Zoey Fools Around
#2 Jake Finds Out
#3 Nina Won't Tell
#4 Ben's In Love
#5 Claire Gets Caught
#6 What Zoey Saw
#7 Lucas Gets Hurt
#8 Aisha Goes Wild

BONFIRE

Katherine Applegate

HarperPaperbacks

A Division of HarperCollins*Publishers*

HarperPaperbacks   *A Division of* HarperCollins*Publishers*
10 East 53rd Street, New York, N.Y. 10022

Produced by Daniel Weiss Associates, Inc., 33 West 17th Street, New York, New York 10011.

First printing: September 1994

Printed in the United States of America

HarperPaperbacks and colophon are trademarks of HarperCollins*Publishers*

10 9 8 7 6 5 4 3 2 1

Many thanks to Liana Cassel for her work in preparing this manuscript.

ONE

There had been ceiling lights, Marta remembered. She had seen them through half-open eyes. Like white lines on a highway, over and over. And dark heads, leaning down above her, blocking the lights. They were talking to her, yelling at her. *What did I do wrong?* she kept trying to ask, but she could only cry.

Above her floated her father's face. Luis Salgado. His eyes were red, his forehead creased. His mouth kept opening and closing, but she couldn't hear him. *Something's wrong, something's wrong,* she tried to say. *I'm in trouble.* But she saw no change in his face. His lips just kept moving and moving, and she knew that he was praying. She was afraid for the first time. *Help me!* her mind screamed as her father's face grew blurry.

Where is Christina? Marta wanted to ask him. *What happened to my friend?*

Marta remembered the paramedics lifting her from the school steps. When they picked her up, she turned her head and saw Christina, still crumpled against the school door. Her sweater was full of holes. There was blood on her clothes. Someone was carrying a sheet, and they dropped it on Christina's head—

What about me? Marta suddenly thought. She remembered the feel of the bullet exploding into her back. She was thrown forward onto the school steps, staring at Christina's white face. Lying with her cheek on the cold cement, her body was numb. All she sensed was a dampness around her waist.

In the emergency room Marta tried to raise her head. She wanted to see what had happened to her, but they stopped her. The nurses and doctors. Their hands were everywhere. The lights above her were in her eyes. Marta had to squint, and the white figures were blurry outlines. They took off her clothes, touching her everywhere. She felt like a rag doll.

A mask was lowered onto her face. Two strong hands held her head down onto the pillow. She saw scissors and heard the sound of ripping clothes. Then she saw pieces of her jeans. One pants leg passing over her, torn and bloody.

2

And then the other leg, her socks, her underwear. They were cutting with the scissors, cutting at her clothes, cutting at her. Then she didn't feel anything.

Slowly Marta opened her eyes and tore herself from the painful flashback. But she couldn't shake off the feelings of confusion and terror. Especially when she looked around. She was in a hospital.

The room was white and cool, and smelled of disinfectant. There were hushed noises from the hall: men and women moving past in soft-soled shoes, gurneys rolling by on well-greased wheels. A low steady beep came from some machinery in the corner.

"You're not in that bed anymore," Marta reminded herself.

But you're still in your chair, her mind responded before she could stop the thought.

Her hands clutched at the smooth steel rails of her wheelchair. She rolled herself closer to the bed and looked at its sleeping occupant.

Dominic Velasquez lay beneath the sheet. All of the vibrant, almost dangerous, strength he exuded was gone. His ink-black hair was pushed off his face, and his dark skin had lost all its color. His face was incredibly pale, almost ghostly white. His eyes were closed, ringed by deep purple marks of weakness and exhaustion. His hands were crossed limply over his chest.

Only hours ago he'd been wheeled into the operating room at the clinic where Marta worked. When she'd recognized him, Marta had frozen. And the two paramedics, strangers, had shouted at her as they moved to save his unconscious, bloody body. The paramedics had pushed her out of the way, and she'd stayed in the corner, a silent statue, watching them work on Dominic. The scissor that tore away his shirt. The forceps with cotton gauze soaked bright red as the paramedics tried to stem the flow of blood from the knife wound in Dominic's stomach.

It had all happened so fast. One minute Marta had been laughing with Justin in the waiting room of the clinic. The next she was here at the main hospital, where Dominic had been transferred after the paramedics were able to stabilize his condition in the clinic emergency room.

Marta glanced at Dominic. It looked as though he was barely breathing. It was good that he was still unconscious, Marta knew. He would need all the rest he could get to survive the trauma and shock. And when the anesthesia and the painkillers wore off, it would be hard for him to get the sleep he would need.

Marta thought of the last time she had seen

Dominic. It had been just yesterday morning on the boardwalk. Dominic had told her that he was leaving town. He'd said he would never see her again. But now, here he was. So close that Marta could reach out and touch him.

"Come on, honey. You've got to tell us the truth. Now, what happened?" the cop said, holding his pad ready, a pen in his hand.

Roan Prentice was on the couch in the hospital waiting room. She sat with her feet up, hugging her knees with her thin arms. Above her, to both sides, stood Ocean City policemen. She stared at her arms, at the pale-blond hair on them sticky and matted with blood. Her hands and fingers were red, her jeans and T-shirt still streaked with blood.

"Are you sure you don't want to go wash up first?" the younger of the two policemen asked.

Roan looked at him blankly. Weren't there always two policemen? Roan wondered. Good-cop and Bad-cop, that was what you called them. But which one was which?

"The bathroom, young lady?" the cop with the pad snapped. "You want to give us an answer or are we supposed to read your mind?"

That's definitely Bad-cop, Roan thought. Roan shook her head in answer.

"Okay," the cop with the pad continued, "so

that's a no. Can we start now?" He coughed loudly into his hand. "You said there was a man who grabbed you."

"Rick." Roan's voice was barely a whisper as she said the name.

"Rick Masters?" the young cop asked.

"I don't know his last name," Roan replied.

"And just how long," Bad-cop asked snidely, "have you known Mr. Masters—I mean, Rick?"

"I haven't known him," Roan answered. "I just met him today."

"And he threatened you? Just like that?"

"Yes." Her voice was a whisper. "I had a bus ticket, to go see my grandma." Roan looked up. "She lives in Kansas. I was going to live with her. And then he tried to stop me. He said—" She shook her head.

"What did he say?" the young cop asked softly.

"He said he knew I didn't have any more money," Roan continued, her voice shaky. "And he had a way for me to earn some."

The policemen looked at each other.

"Roan," the young cop said. "Mr. Masters told us something else. He had a very different story. He said you were at his house today. He said you wanted money from him, that you propositioned him. He said you had offered to sleep with him, among other things, to get this money. And he also told us that when he refused, you stole from him. He said that you stole the money you used to buy your bus ticket."

"No!" Roan cried, shaking her head violently. "No, it's not true. Nothing he said is true. It was my own money. I didn't take anything from him. *He* wanted . . . he had friends there, two of them, and they had a camera . . . they said I knew . . . but I didn't—" Her voice caught, and she began choking back sobs. "I didn't steal anything. I climbed out the bathroom window—"

"And you went to the station?"

"I bought a ticket, and I was going to go," she said, her breath coming fast and short. "But then he was there, and he grabbed me, and I ran away. And then he . . ." She nodded down the hospital corridor, toward the room where Dominic was lying unconscious. "He came from the bathroom, and he grabbed me."

"He grabbed you too?" Good-cop asked.

"Yes." Roan nodded. "I ran into him. And he had a knife—"

"Dominic—" the cops said together.

"No, no," Roan said vehemently. "The other one. Rick. Rick had a knife, and he was going to— he was coming at me—and then I ran into Dominic, and he grabbed me and pushed me away, and then I fell, and I heard people screaming." Roan was reliving the awful scene in her mind. "And then I crawled on the floor and saw Dominic—and he had the knife in his stomach, and there was blood everywhere, and I was going to pull it out, but he said no."

"He wouldn't let you take the knife out?" Bad-cop asked.

"No," Roan said. "He said it would be worse to take it out. Then he would bleed to death and it was better to leave it there until the ambulance came. He said I was shaking so much, he was afraid I would cut him with it worse. And then he laughed."

"Roan," Bad-cop said impatiently, "there's something you're not telling us. Now, we're trying to be nice, but you're not telling us the truth. Why did you go to Mr. Masters's house?"

"A friend," Roan said. "A friend told me to go. I just needed a place to stay—"

"Why?" Good-cop interrupted. "Because you were in trouble?"

"No—" Roan shook her head.

"What kind of trouble were you in, Roan?" Bad-cop demanded. "If you already had the money, why didn't you go straight to the bus station?"

"Because I wasn't going to leave—" she whispered.

"Until you'd robbed Mr. Masters, you mean," Bad-cop said.

"No!" Roan cried. "Until he tried to—he was

going to—I just wanted a place to stay for a few days, but then he—I needed to get away," Roan explained, hugging her knees tighter and starting to rock back and forth. "And so I ran to the station, and thought of my grandma—"

"You mean, thought *up* your grandma?" Bad-cop said.

"No, no. She's real!" Roan cried. "She's real and she was always nice to me. I know she would remember—"

"And we know you can remember, Roan," Bad-cop warned, cutting her off. "And we need you to remember." He paused. "And you need yourself to remember—that is, if you don't want to find yourself in jail for solicitation or theft."

"What do you mean, jail?" Roan whispered, her eyes wide with fear. She turned to the young cop, Good-cop.

"Roan," he said, his eyes narrowing on hers. "If you were worried about what Rick Masters wanted to do with you, you'd better start answering our questions truthfully. From what I know, it will be nothing compared to the way you'll worry in women's prison."

"What!" Roan gasped. "Someone tried to kill me and you're going to put *me* in jail? I can't believe this."

"Believe it," Bad-cop said. "Now tell us what happened."

9

Roan pushed her hands against her seat and tried to stand. "Listen," she said shakily, "I need to go to the bathroom now—"

"Sit down!" Bad-cop barked, pushing her roughly back onto the couch.

"But—"

"Get out the handcuffs," Bad-cop snapped. The young policeman drew a pair of handcuffs from his back pocket. Roan watched him in horror as he twisted the key and popped them open.

"You can't go anywhere unless we say you can," the young cop explained. "So you'd better listen to my partner. And you'd better tell him the truth."

"But I told the truth," Roan said. *And I thought you were the good one,* she thought.

"Then you'll have to tell us again, until we believe you."

"Or we can take you in right now," Bad-cop suggested.

"You can't," Roan whispered.

"Oh yes we can," the young cop said softly.

Roan looked back and forth at the two men standing above her. She felt like she was on trial. The police were acting like *she'd* done something wrong.

"Don't I get a phone call?" she asked, her voice shaking.

"That's after we arrest you," Bad-cop said. "Are you saying we should arrest you? Is it a lawyer you want to call?"

Roan shook her head. "Please," she begged. "I don't want you to arrest me. Can I please make a phone call now?"

Two

Kate Quinn limped up the stairs to her room. Her foot was starting to throb again, and she wondered if there was any way she could get her hands on some painkillers. *Don't be a baby,* she said to herself. She was embarrassed about how she'd gotten her wound—jumping down from her lifeguarding chair onto a shell and cutting her foot.

Some big savior she'd turned out to be. The damsel in distress wasn't the girl Kate had heard screaming. That girl was being tickled by her boyfriend. The one who ended up screaming, who ended up surrounded by concerned men in tiny bathing suits, was Kate herself.

"I guess the pretty lifeguard needs some lifeguarding," Kate had heard someone say behind her.

Well, so much for women's liberation. She'd probably set it back by at least a day with that mishap.

And if the truth were known, it wasn't just her foot that Kate was embarrassed about. She had just spent what may have been some of the most uncomfortable minutes of her life watching Marta and Justin Garrett together at the clinic, where she'd gone to get fixed up.

Kate sighed. What was wrong with her? She was the one who had told Justin that their relationship was over. She was the one who'd said they had no future together. And yet she was also the one who found it hard to see him with someone else. Especially someone she knew. And liked.

Justin's old girlfriend, Grace Caywood, had started out as Kate's enemy. Now they were becoming real friends. But Marta was already Kate's friend. What would this do to their relationship?

"It shouldn't *do* anything," Kate told herself angrily. "You're not fighting over the same guy anymore. You have your own guy this summer. All your own."

Kate smiled. Tosh McCall was what kept her out of the whole situation this summer. Wonderful Tosh. Dependable Tosh. *My lover.* Kate turned red at the thought, and almost giggled. Still, it just seemed too awkward to have to think about. All of them living together, and Justin across the street. Ugh!

Poor Tosh, Kate thought. How amazing he'd been to her all this time. What a situation to walk into. But he'd stuck it out. He'd said he loved her, and he'd proved it. He'd stayed through everything. He would give her a hug and tell her she was still a great lifeguard, even if she had sensitive feet. Kate reached out and turned the knob of her bedroom door.

No, no, this isn't your room, a voice said to her as her mouth fell open in shock. *You must have gone to the wrong house. All these contemporary wooden homes look the same, don't they? Anybody could make this mistake. But you should definitely leave these people alone before they notice you.*

Kate was about to back away and close the door when she glanced around the room and saw the clothes hanging in the closet. *Oh, wait a minute,* the voice said. *Isn't that your blue striped dress? The nice one that Chelsea's always borrowing? And there are your hiking boots on the floor, still covered with dirt. You really should clean them off, you know.*

"This is my room," Kate finally whispered. She was horrified. And she realized that getting a hug from Tosh was going to be very hard. Someone else, a girl Kate had never seen before, had beaten her to it. Kate felt sick.

"I don't believe what I'm seeing," she said.

The girl must have heard Kate speak, because she looked up and saw Kate over Tosh's shoulder, and froze. Tosh muttered something and lifted himself from her.

"Sandy—?" Kate heard him say. He began to turn his head. She knew that in a few seconds she would be looking at him. He would see her standing there, in the doorway of her own room. Kate wished the ground would open up and swallow her.

Tosh turned, and their eyes met. Then Kate's throat loosened up.

"Get out of my bed!" she shouted.

Instantly the girl leapt to her feet and began scrambling for her clothes. Kate watched her as though it were all happening in slow motion. Strangely enough, Kate realized that the girl looked familiar. It was on the tip of her tongue to ask where they'd met. Somewhere. Kate had seen her before. But the girl's nakedness seemed to distract Kate's powers of recognition.

Kate watched as the girl stumbled into a pair of flowery shorts, grabbed a shirt from the floor, and rushed past Kate down the stairs.

Kate turned back to the bed and saw that Tosh hadn't moved. She looked away quickly.

"Get out," she demanded, her eyes fixed on the

wall. Kate didn't want to look at him. She didn't want to see him there, lying naked in her bed.

"Kate—" he began.

"Get out!" she screamed. "I mean it. Out!"

In the distance Kate heard a phone begin its insistent wail.

Chelsea's shirt was sticking to her back.

"Ugh," she cried, picking her clothes away from her body. "I feel like I'm wearing Saran Wrap in a microwave."

Chelsea clutched her big sketch pad under her arm. Pencils were bunched in her fist and poking out from every available pocket. She was returning from a long morning of sketching on the boardwalk.

Earlier, in the amusement park, she had found a couple that she particularly liked—a young couple, probably close to her age. She'd loved the way they were dressed. The girl had been wearing ankle boots and a short sundress with a flaring skirt.

Chelsea had followed them around like a detective. Or a journalist. *That's right,* she'd thought to herself, ducking behind a pyramid of stuffed elephants with a small sketch pad in her hand. She was Chelsea Lennox, Investigative Artist.

She'd had lots of fun doing quick sketches of

the couple, and her sketchbook read like a story; first they'd walked around and looked at everything, then they'd bought some lunch, played a few games, won a rubber snake that the boy wore around his neck, had a fight, and made up. Those were the sketches Chelsea liked the best—the making up—and she had to admit that her little black pencil drawings came out very romantic.

Chelsea's face felt hot, and she knew that another hour or so in the sun would have given her a full-blown sunburn. Not that anyone else ever really noticed when she got a burn. Or a tan, for that matter. But she felt it. And a sunburn was never fun. She never would have believed she would ever complain about spending too many hours in the sun, but today she almost longed for a cool air-conditioned studio to work in. Almost.

Chelsea looked up as she neared the house, and she saw Grace walking up the path to the front door.

"Hey, Grace," Chelsea called, "slow down a second." Chelsea caught up to her as they reached the landing.

"Have any luck finding Roan?" Chelsea asked, out of breath from her quick jog.

Grace's face clouded over, and she shook her head. "I didn't see her anywhere this morning while I was checking on my beach stands."

17

Grace sighed. "I can't bear the thought of calling the police," she admitted. "It's like I'd be sending dogs after her or something."

"Has Bo come back?" Chelsea asked softly as Grace pushed open the front door.

Grace just shook her head.

"I'm sorry," Chelsea replied. "I didn't mean to remind—"

Suddenly they heard a scream. A moment later a figure streaked down the stairs.

A half-naked girl pushed between them, holding her clothes to her chest, and sprinted out the door.

Grace and Chelsea watched the stranger run up the walk, and then turned to each other.

"Have you ever—?" Chelsea began.

"Who in the name of—?" Grace asked.

They heard yelling from upstairs, and they both moved to the stairway. Then the phone began to ring.

"It might be—" Grace began, looking back toward the kitchen.

"I'll get it," Chelsea said, stepping off the stairs and pushing Grace up.

Chelsea dropped her sketch pad and pencils on the living-room rug and turned back to the kitchen. She snatched the phone from its cradle.

"Yes, what?" she snapped.

"Kate?" a small voice came through the line.

"No, it's Chelsea. Who's this?"

"Chelsea," the voice choked. "It's Roan."

"Roan! Where are you?"

Roan started sobbing on the other end of the line.

"Roan? Roan? Are you there? What's wrong?" Chelsea asked.

"I'm here," she sobbed. "At the hospital. With the police. He tried to kill me, I think—"

"What!" Chelsea shrieked. "Kill you? Who's trying to kill you?"

"He had a knife, but Dominic was there, and he stabbed him." Roan's voice crackled.

"Who?" Chelsea cried. "Who stabbed who?"

"He stabbed Dominic," Roan choked out. "And the police are here, and they're going to take me away. Please, get Grace. Please, please tell her to come. I don't know what they're going to do."

"You're at the hospital?" Chelsea asked. "Okay. Stay there. Don't move. I'm with Grace. I'll bring her right over."

Tosh was moving toward her, his arms out as if he were comforting a frightened child.

"Kate, Kate," he was whispering, "you don't understand. Kate, honey, be quiet now and let me explain. It's not what you think."

"It's not what I think?" Kate asked incredulously. "Are you kidding me? What are you going

19

to try and tell me—this is summer session for you? You're tutoring classes in sex ed? Do you really think I'm that stupid?"

"Kate, please," Tosh was pleading. "Don't get hysterical. Just calm down."

"Calm down?" Kate snapped. "Don't get hysterical? You're in my bed with someone else and I can't get hysterical?"

"Kate, please." Tosh moved toward her. "You've got to relax and—"

"You've got to put some clothes on," Kate cried in disgust. "I can't believe this. If I wasn't so mad I'd be laughing. You want to try and defend yourself and you're still standing in the middle of my room with no clothes on!"

Tosh blushed and turned away, snatching at his shorts and pulling them on, along with a rumpled gray T-shirt.

"Kate," Tosh said, turning back to her, "listen. You've got to listen to me. I can explain this."

"I don't think you can explain it," Kate said. "I don't think I need it *explained*. I know what I saw, Tosh. Believe me, I *know*."

"Kate, there are some things you don't understand—" Tosh said.

"Don't patronize me," she snapped. "I understand. I learned about the birds and the bees a long time ago."

"Kate, it's not the birds and the bees," Tosh

said. "It's more complicated than that."

"No, Tosh," Kate answered. "What would have been more complicated was finding another place to have your little fling. Doesn't she have a home? You had to come here and do that in my own bed? Suddenly I'm beginning to feel you're much less intelligent than I gave you credit for."

"And much more sleazy than anyone would have believed," Grace added from the doorway.

Kate looked at her quickly, already feeling embarrassment. Even if they were becoming friends, Grace wouldn't have been the person Kate picked to witness this scene. But Grace sent her a tight smile, and her eyes were hard, not in amusement but in anger. Suddenly Kate realized that Grace might not be the friendliest person in the world, but she was loyal.

"Listen, Grace," Tosh said, turning to her. "I appreciate the concern, but this doesn't have anything to do with you."

"What's wrong, Tosh?" Grace asked, leaning against the doorjamb. "Can't take an audience? I thought you were used to working in front of a crowd, as a teacher of course."

"Grace," Tosh said tightly, "this is a private matter."

"Right," she sighed. "That's just what that girl said as she was running out the front door."

"Grace—" Tosh went to move toward her, but Kate put her hand out against his chest.

"Tosh," she said sharply. "I don't need you to tell my friends what to do. I already told you to leave myself." Tosh turned to her and Kate involuntarily took a step backward, landing on her injured foot and sucking in her breath.

"What happened to you?" Tosh asked, looking down at the bandage she wore.

"At the moment, I don't think you're really in a position to act concerned for my welfare," Kate replied. "I suggest you do me the courtesy of leaving me alone. I think I deserve at least that much."

Tosh stepped back and considered her. For a moment, Kate wondered if he would go, and then she wondered what she would do next if he didn't. But he seemed to decide that the time wasn't ripe for conversation. He took his sunglasses from the bedside table, pulled a light jacket from a hanger in the closet, and walked past her without saying a word.

When he got to the door, he paused, as if to say something to Grace.

"Tough luck, pal," Grace spoke first. "Getting caught does tarnish the reputation, doesn't it? But of course," she went on sweetly as she moved aside to let him pass, "it doesn't have anything to do with me, so how would I know?"

Kate watched him stiffen and leave. She listened to the sound of his feet on the stairs. Grace turned to her, and Kate waved her hand quickly.

"I'd say thanks for being here," Kate said softly, "but I wouldn't mean it."

Grace shrugged. "I wouldn't either," she replied.

"I feel like an idiot."

"It may not mean anything to you," Grace replied, "but you don't look like one. You look pretty in control."

"Don't let it fool you," Kate said, her voice catching. "It's only the calm before the storm."

"Kate!" Chelsea cried, walking into the room. "What's happening? Are you okay?"

"Where's Tosh?" Grace asked calmly.

"I don't know," Chelsea replied. "I didn't see him. Was he here? What was the screaming?"

"Tosh was here," Kate said weakly. "With another woman."

"What?" Chelsea asked. "You mean with that girl we saw? Tosh? Oh, Kate, I'm so sorry, but I—" Chelsea shrugged and dropped her arms. "Kate, listen, I really am sorry," Chelsea said again. "This is just too much for my brain to handle at one time. Don't think I don't know that this is serious, but I have other news I've got to tell you both. That was Roan on the phone."

"Roan?" Grace asked. "Where is she?"

"She's at the hospital, Grace," Chelsea blurted

23

out. "There was a knifing or something. I couldn't understand—"

"Oh my God—" Kate and Grace spoke at the same time.

"Bo—?" Grace asked shakily, her face white.

"No." Chelsea shook her head. "And not Roan, either, I think, but she's really upset. It was Dominic. Someone stabbed him and Roan was there, and now they're all at the hospital. With the police!"

THREE

Grace pulled up to the hospital emergency entrance and parked her car between two idle ambulances.

"Grace," Chelsea asked hesitantly, "are you sure you can park here?"

"No," Grace said, turning off the engine and jumping out of the little BMW. "But if there's an emergency, they can take this. They'll get where they're going much faster."

Grace led the way into the emergency room.

"Excuse me," Grace said, stopping a nurse rushing past her. "We're looking for our friends. There was a knifing, a man and a young blond girl?"

"Oh yes. He was here, but he's gone now," the nurse replied. "I think they've moved him to second-floor observation."

They got directions from the nurse at reception and headed to the elevators.

"I hate hospitals," Chelsea whispered, walking close to Kate, her sandals slipping on the polished tiled floors. "I can't believe someone got stabbed in Ocean City! This is the kind of thing that's only supposed to happen in New York."

"Chelsea, you sound like my parents," Kate replied.

"Yeah, I know. I sound like mine, too."

"That's not what would bother me if I was hurt here," Grace said, jabbing at the elevator button.

"What *would* bother you, Grace?" Chelsea asked.

The doors opened, and Grace walked into the elevator and turned around. "Can't you see?" Grace asked sarcastically. "This is just the place I'd want to be—Ocean City Hospital for a stab wound."

"Right," Kate said. "What do you think they're used to here? Third-degree sunburn?"

"Broken seashells?" Grace added.

"Don't forget about Jaws," Chelsea warned.

"How many shark attacks do you think they have here?" Grace asked, almost laughing.

"I don't know," Chelsea replied. "How many knifings are there?"

"Good point," Grace acknowledged, her face suddenly stonelike.

"We don't even know what happened yet, Grace," Kate said. "Why don't you find out before you start feeling responsible."

"If Roan is in trouble, I am responsible," Grace replied as the elevator doors opened. "What's the point of denying it?"

She stepped out of the elevator and paused. Across the room she saw two uniformed policemen in front of a couch. She glimpsed a shock of bleached-blond hair. Roan.

My God, Grace thought as she got close enough to see Roan clearly. *I hope none of that is her blood.*

"I'm Grace Caywood," Grace said smoothly. She put out her hand to the two cops.

"Miss Caywood," the older policeman said, nodding. "We have a few questions for you if you don't mind." Grace smiled stiffly as he continued. "Miss Prentice says she lives with you and that you are her employer. Is this true?"

Grace looked at Roan and couldn't help remembering the scene in the living room last night. Roan and Bo had come home drunk, and Grace had laid into Roan. This morning she'd been gone.

"Yes, it is," Grace responded calmly. "May I ask why she looks like she's walked off a horror-movie set? Couldn't you let her go to the bathroom to wash up?"

"We tried," the young cop answered, "but she didn't want to move."

"Roan?" Grace said, turning to her. "Would you like to go to the bathroom to wash up?"

Roan nodded.

"It looks like she wants to move now," Grace said sweetly.

"You can take her in a minute," the older cop said.

"Look," the young cop explained. "There's no reason for you to get upset here. We're just doing our job. A man was almost killed, Miss Caywood. And this young lady was involved in that. Obviously she's afraid. When people are afraid, Miss Caywood—"

"Listen, I know what people do when they're afraid," Grace cut him off. "And I doubt you're making it any better for her. Is she in trouble or not?"

"Well, we have someone in custody right now who claims that Miss Prentice stole some money from him."

"I'm sure she didn't," Grace replied. She looked at Roan again. "She's not a thief," Grace snapped. "And anyway, is this 'someone in custody' the one with the knife? Would that give this 'someone in custody' the right to go after her with it?"

"Of course not, Miss Caywood," the younger cop replied. "Look, she's not under arrest. But we will need to corroborate her story with the young man who was stabbed. And we will need her to come down to the station to identify the assailant."

"Fine," Grace answered, reaching into her bag and pulling out a business card. "Here's where she'll be staying. You can call me first."

Kate followed Chelsea down the hall, peeking into the small windows on the doors of all the rooms. She felt sort of gruesome peering in at everyone, especially when they turned to see who was looking at them. Kate felt like she was at the zoo looking for a particular animal. *Nope, not the one with the broken leg. Not the one on the respirator. We're here for the stabbing victim.* She was relieved when Chelsea finally whispered they'd found him.

When Kate looked through the tiny window on Dominic's door, she saw Marta wheeled up next to his bed. She was staring off at the blank wall, her eyes glazed over as if she were in a trance.

Chelsea tapped softly on the door and opened it a crack.

"Marta," she whispered into the room. "Marta?"

Suddenly Kate saw Marta jerk up in her chair and turn to them. Her eyes focused, and her face grew red. She lifted a finger to her lips and motioned that she would come out to the hall. Chelsea let the door close, and they stepped back. Kate sighed. What was she going to say? The last time she saw Marta . . .

"Boy," Chelsea whispered to Kate. "She must be freaking out. I know she said she wasn't seeing him anymore, but this—"

Chelsea let the sentence hang. Kate had only found out about Marta and Justin a few hours ago herself. She was sure Chelsea didn't know anything about it yet.

"Chelsea," Kate began, "there's something you don't know."

"What?"

"About Marta. I was at the clinic earlier—"

Just then the door to Dominic's room opened, and Marta wheeled herself into the corridor.

"Marta." Chelsea rushed over to her. "Is he okay? Roan told me a little bit on the phone. I can't believe it!"

"He's all right," Marta replied, glancing quickly at Kate and then looking away. "I was at the clinic when the ambulance brought him. It was touch and go for a while, but he's stabilized now."

"What happened?" Kate asked.

"Some guy was after Roan for something," Marta explained. "I'm not exactly sure, but he pulled a knife on her, and Dominic was there to get in the way of it."

"Roan seems to have a lot of friends who carry knives," Chelsea remarked. "Remember that kid at Justin's service on the beach?" Chelsea shivered and made a face. "It's still so weird to talk about it like that now that he's alive."

"Yeah," Kate and Marta said together. "But apparently this time Dominic wasn't able to take it away from the guy so easily," Marta finished.

Kate and Chelsea exchanged glances.

"Anyway," Marta sighed, "I don't think this was one of Roan's friends."

"How are you holding up?" Chelsea asked.

"I'm fine," Marta said coldly.

"But what about Dominic?" Chelsea pressed. "I mean, you must feel terrible. If there's anything we can do—"

"Of course it's terrible," Marta snapped. "Violence is always terrible. No one ever deserves it."

"Of course not," Chelsea said quickly. "That's not what I meant."

"Sure I feel terrible," Marta continued, "but it's not my problem."

Kate watched Chelsea's mouth open and

close. Kate could practically read her mind. *What did I say wrong?* Chelsea was thinking. Chelsea looked over at her in confusion, and Kate shrugged her shoulders. Then she nodded over her shoulder at the bathrooms at the end of the hall.

"Marta?" Chelsea asked. "You'll be here in a minute?"

Marta nodded at them absently, hardly aware of their leaving.

When they got into the bathroom, Chelsea grabbed Kate.

"What is wrong with her?" Chelsea squeaked.

Kate sighed. "I don't know for sure," she said. "But I didn't get a chance to tell you. The reason I was home before is because I hurt my foot at work, and when I went to the clinic earlier, I saw Marta there."

"Your foot?" Chelsea said. "The clinic? What happened to you? What's happening to everyone?" Chelsea's voice rose hysterically.

Kate smiled and grabbed her friend by the shoulder. "It's all right, Chelsea. It's one of those days. I just cut it on a shell at the beach, but that's not important. When I was at the clinic I saw Marta, and when I was leaving I saw Justin there too."

"Justin? Did he know you'd hurt yourself?"

Kate shook her head. "He wasn't there to see

me," Kate explained. "It was pretty awful timing that I was there, actually. He was there to see Marta. They went out together on Friday night. And he was there to take her to lunch."

"Justin and Marta?"

Kate nodded. "They're dating now . . . I think. So you'd better lay off the 'Oh, Dominic' stuff."

"But Justin?" Chelsea shook her head. "I never would have thought—" Then Chelsea stopped and looked at Kate closely. "Why are you telling me this so calmly? You're talking about it like you don't care."

Kate shrugged helplessly. "What can I say about it? I'm the one who dumped him, remember? For Mr. Understanding?"

"Oh no, Kate," Chelsea said, smacking her forehead with her hand. "Tosh! I almost forgot about him. You must feel terrible!"

"You're beginning to sound like a broken record," Kate remarked.

"Well, *I* feel terrible," Chelsea wailed. "I don't know why no one else does. Roan runs away, you hurt yourself, Justin is dating Marta, Tosh is sleeping with someone else, and Dominic is stabbed! And my only problem is that my marriage is breaking up! It's like everything is falling apart, and it's all happening today." Chelsea stared around the bathroom. "You know," she said, "I think it's safe in here. I'm not going to leave this bathroom. Ever."

Kate gave Chelsea a quick hug. "Come on, it's not that bad."

Chelsea gave her a look.

"Not bad enough to spend the rest of your life in a bathroom, anyway. I mean, at least you can pick a bathroom with a Jacuzzi and a sauna in it. You deserve some pleasures."

Chelsea giggled. "How can you have a sense of humor right now?"

"I don't know," Kate admitted. "You're right. I do feel awful. I'm just trying not to think about it. One tragedy at a time, and stab wounds take precedence, okay?"

"Okay," Chelsea responded wearily. "What comes after that?"

"Let's worry about that later," Kate replied. "After we deal with Dominic and Roan." But silently she completed her list: Stab wounds first. Then two-timing boyfriend. After that, she'd worry about the rest of the summer.

"Let's get out of here," Kate said, tugging Chelsea out the door.

Grace pulled Roan into the nearby bathroom and turned to face her. Roan's hair was wild and tangled, matted with blood where she'd run her hands through it. She had brown stains all over her jeans and the bottom of her T-shirt. Dried blood. Grace shuddered. She hadn't been kidding when she told the cops that Roan looked like she'd walked off the set of a horror movie.

"You look like hell," Grace said. She reached out to push Roan's hair from her face, but Roan flinched away.

"What do you think I'm going to do?" Grace asked. "Hit you?"

"You wanted to last night," Roan answered, staring down at the floor.

Grace sighed. *Well,* she thought, *I can't argue with that. I certainly did. Then.*

"Yeah, well, we all lose our temper sometimes," Grace answered. "Why don't you wash yourself off. You're really giving me the creeps."

Roan turned on the taps in the faucet and began soaping the dried blood from her hands. Grace watched her, her movements slow and careful.

"Why did you tell them that I was staying with you?" Roan asked.

"Who, the police?" Grace asked, looking away. This wasn't the Roan she was used to, Grace thought. No more in-your-face attitude. No more snotty confrontations. Then again, even Grace might not have much attitude after going through what Roan had just experienced.

"You're not going anywhere today, are you?" Grace asked.

Roan shook her head.

"Then it's true for now, isn't it?" Grace said. "Besides, you've already gotten me in enough trouble with my brother."

Roan looked up and caught Grace's eye in the mirror.

"What do you mean?" she asked.

He called me a hypocrite, Grace thought to herself. *He thinks he can't depend on me anymore.* She shook her head.

"I've had to identify enough bodies in my life," she replied instead, trying to sound calm. "It's not really my goal to make yours another one."

Roan wiped her hands on a paper towel and tried to smooth down her hair.

"Are you finished?" Grace asked. "We'll talk later, all right?"

They left the bathroom and walked over to Marta, Kate, and Chelsea.

"Is Dominic all right?" Grace asked.

Marta nodded.

"Sorry," Grace said to her. "Are you okay?"

"Why is everyone apologizing to me?" Marta snapped.

"Okay, I'm not sorry," Grace replied. "We all

36

have our own way of coping, I guess," she said, looking at Marta strangely.

Just then the elevator doors opened, and Justin came rushing over to the group.

"I'm sorry I'm so late," he said breathlessly, moving to Marta's side. "I got here as soon as I could."

Grace watched him reach out to touch Marta and then hesitate, his hand fluttering for a moment and then dropping back to his side.

"How are you?" Justin asked, turning to Roan. She nodded silently.

"Grace," Justin said in greeting, "Chelsea, Kate." He paused. "How's your foot?" he asked awkwardly.

"Fine," Kate replied, her voice low.

"How's Dominic?" Justin asked, turning to Marta.

"Fine," Marta answered.

Grace looked around at their little circle. Chelsea was chewing on her lip. Marta was staring into her lap. Kate and Justin kept looking at each other and looking away. Roan was sniffling.

"Okay," she announced. "That's it, then. Everyone's fine. Just a local stabbing. Well, you all know how I'd love to stay and be supportive, only nobody here seems to need it, so that lets me off the hook. I'm off." She looked at Kate and Chelsea. "Are you two coming back with me?"

They both nodded.

"Justin? Marta?"

"We'll stay," Justin answered quickly, finally brushing Marta on the elbow with his fingers.

"Okay, then," Grace said lightly. "I guess I'm troop leader. This is shaping up to be one glorious Saturday."

FOUR

"I'm sorry to be such a drag, but I really don't think I want to record this moment for all time," Kate said, staring glumly into her cup of hot tea.

"It's not for all time," Chelsea answered, lowering her sketch pad for a moment. "It's for posterity. Which is a much nicer way of saying for all time. Besides, you look beautiful when you're depressed."

Kate snorted.

"Nice friend you are," she said, looking out over the railing of the balcony to watch the ocean waves roll in.

"I am a nice friend," Chelsea said from behind her pad. "But right now I'm speaking as an artist who doesn't want to lose her model."

Kate smiled and sighed again. Well, she might

as well use this time to review. The stab wounds were a check: Dominic's condition was stable, and Roan wasn't going to jail. That meant it was time to think about Tosh.

Wasn't it only in movies or trashy novels that women found their husbands or boyfriends in bed with other women? Obviously not.

"I can't believe I have to go up there and look at all his *stuff*," Kate sighed.

"Don't think of it that way," Chelsea advised. "Use it as an opportunity to work out some of your anger. Go up there and look at all his stuff that you get to throw out. Or cut up with a pair of scissors. Or burn on the beach."

"Is that what you did with Connor's stuff?" Kate asked.

"No," Chelsea replied softly. "I was the one who left. I threw out, cut up, and burnt my own things."

"I know, Chels. I'm sorry." Kate put down the mug and ran her hands through her hair. "You're right," she growled. "I am angry. I shouldn't snap at you."

"That's okay." Chelsea smiled, holding her drawing up to appraise it. "I can take it. I'm sitting here benefiting from your misery. Nice picture, don't you think?"

"Yeah, nice," Kate said, nodding. "If you want a picture of a doormat. I can't believe myself."

"What do you mean, you can't believe yourself?" Chelsea asked. "You didn't do anything to deserve the way Tosh treated you. Come on, Kate. Admit it. What you can't believe is that someone, anyone, would do that *to you.*"

"It's not just my ego," Kate said defensively. "It has to do with love. And trust. I believed him."

"And you got taken," Chelsea said. "But that's not what makes you mad. What makes you mad is that you weren't enough."

Kate shook her head.

"Well," Chelsea admitted. "That's what makes me mad anyway." Kate was silent for a moment. She glanced over at Chelsea, but Chelsea's head was bent as she examined her drawing. *Poor Chelsea,* Kate thought, for the first time really understanding her pain.

"You're right," Kate said softly. "That is why I'm angry. But that's wrong, too. It's not my fault. It's his. Because I am enough, and he's just not smart enough to see it." Kate stood and turned to the glass doors. "And so are you," she said softly, putting her hand on Chelsea's shoulder and squeezing.

"Where are you going?"

"I'm going upstairs to pack his things," Kate explained. "When I see him again, I want it to be short and painless."

Kate walked up to her room and pushed open the door.

41

"What is this?" Kate demanded. "For the rest of my life, every time I open the door to my room am I going to find you here? How dare you come into my room like this."

"Kate?" Tosh said gently. "Kate, are you okay?"

He was sitting on her bed, looking pitiful and forlorn. He was pouting as though he had spent the morning being unfairly punished. He rose and moved to come toward her. But that seemed to send the right message to Kate's brain.

"Stop!" Kate barked, holding her hand up like a traffic cop. "What the hell are you doing here!"

Tosh stopped in his tracks. He nodded, smiled at her carefully, and backed up onto her bed.

"Kate," he said calmly. "I think we need to talk. And I think you need to try and get a grip on yourself. Now isn't the time for hysterics again."

Kate nodded. This was okay, she could handle this. This was Tosh, slipping into his T.A. role, all calm and intellectual. This was a ploy, but Kate had taken this class in her first semester at college, and it was called psychology; accuse the woman of being hysterical, and anything she says, especially if she gets mad, becomes meaningless.

Kate smiled. Completely serene. Numb was closer to the truth, but it would look the same to Tosh.

"Hysterical?" Kate scoffed. "Why should I be

hysterical?" She gave Tosh a half smile. "Just because you're living with me, because you told me that you loved me and I found you in my bed with someone else? Why on earth would that make me hysterical?"

"Okay, Kate," Tosh answered, "there's no reason to be flip about it. I get the sarcasm. And I know you deserve an explanation. And if you let me, I'll be able to give you one."

"I'm anxious to hear it," Kate replied. "Only because I've always known how smart you were. Now I'll get to see how imaginative."

"Kate," Tosh snapped angrily, "you're not being fair. You already think I'm lying. Can't you even give me the courtesy of listening?"

"Are you getting hysterical?" Kate asked, her voice full of mock concern. "I certainly don't want you to get hysterical. I know how anxious hysterical people can be."

"Kate," he moaned, "how can you do this to me? Don't you understand how hard it's been for me? Not just this last week, but these last five or six months?" Tosh's voice was a pleading one, and when Kate looked closely at him, she saw that his face looked truly pained.

"First I had to wait an entire semester for our class to finish before I could ask you out," Tosh continued. "Then I had to compete with an ex-boyfriend who had left you to sail around the world with his ex-girlfriend. Then I had to compete with his ghost. And *then,* just when it seems that I finally," he sighed heavily and lifted his hands, "finally have you to myself, he comes back to life, and wants to waltz back into a relationship with you as if he hasn't done anything wrong."

Tosh rose and started toward her again. This time Kate was silent.

"Kate, I was there for you the whole time." Tosh reached out and put a hand on her shoulder. "Kate, I was the one who saw you feeling rejected by him. I was the one who saw you grieving for him. I was the one who was there, always, wanting to be there. And after all of that, I have to find him living right across the street, and I feel like I'm fighting it all over again, that I'm fighting for you all over again."

Kate closed her eyes, trying to turn away from his voice. It was true that Tosh had been there for her. It was true that she had given him a very hard time, that she had treated him terribly, that she had been unable for so long to give him anything because of the shadow Justin had cast over her heart.

"How can you expect it to be easy for me when you know all along that you've been fighting your own feelings?" he asked softly, his breath stirring her hair.

Kate winced. She had been tempted, especially that night she'd met Justin on the beach.

"You think I don't see it, Kate." Tosh's voice was low and pained. "You think it doesn't hurt me. But now, when you see how much it hurts me, instead of trying to help me, instead of standing by me like I stood by you, you're ready to throw me out."

Kate sighed. She didn't know what she felt. Somehow the anger had been drained from her by Tosh's words. So much of what he'd said was true.

Suddenly Kate's eyes flew open and she sucked in her breath. *What a snake!* She pushed Tosh away violently.

"I can't believe you tried to do that to me," Kate hissed at him. "Talking about Justin as if it matters what *he's* done to me. The point is what *you've* done to me, Tosh," Kate said slowly. "And you betrayed me. Right here. In my own room. And I saw you with my own eyes. You can't talk that away."

Tosh stepped back from her, and his eyes hardened.

"Maybe I've had feelings, Tosh. Feelings are sometimes very difficult things. But they aren't the same as actions." Kate glared back at him. "I've never cheated on you. And if you've suddenly forgotten how long you pressured me, I was the one who refused to get together with you until I thought I was over Justin, remember? Obviously your memory has lapsed. Along with some other things."

Kate crossed her arms and glared at him. "You have anything to say now?" she challenged him.

"Kate," Tosh sighed, shaking his head. "Kate, it didn't mean anything—"

"Ha!" Kate snorted. "That's the best you can do?"

"Kate—"

"Get out," Kate cut him off. "I'm very calm right now, so you'd better listen to me. Get out. Get out of my room. Get out of my house. Get out of my life."

"Just like that?" Tosh asked.

Kate nodded. "Just like that," she said softly, and she watched him turn away and close the door. Then she stumbled over to her bed and sat down.

First, stab wound. Stab wound, check.

Second, two-timing boyfriend; Tosh had betrayed her and she couldn't forgive him. She realized suddenly that she didn't want to. All along he'd been pushing at her, all along when she thought he'd been there as a friend. Well, he was gone. Out of her life for good. Two-timing boyfriend, check.

Her mind clicked on in its normally efficient

manner, though she didn't want it to. Now, it reminded her, now there's the rest of the summer. And finally Kate started to cry.

Grace was in the kitchen, circling the refrigerator as though it were an enemy and she was deciding on the best way to attack. It looked harmless. Clean and white. Only the best, Grace thought wryly, conjuring a picture of her mother strolling through the house dictating to the interior decorator.

"A refrigerator *with* an automatic ice maker," her mother had probably said. "An automatic ice maker and ice-water dispenser."

Ellen Caywood had always been a fan of automatic ice. It was the only way that she had been able to keep up with her drinking. Grace remembered her mother always leaving the room to go to the kitchen, remembered listening to the grinding sound of the ice maker, the sound of fresh ice cubes clinking into her mother's glass.

Grace dragged her hands through her hair. Going to the hospital had completely unnerved her: finding Roan with those policemen, covered in blood, looking like a deer caught in someone's headlights.

All because of my little show last night, Grace thought. *Because I had to show her who was boss. Because I had to show Bo who was boss.*

"But I just don't want him to make the mistakes *I* made," Grace whispered to herself.

You can't do it with rules like that, she answered. *Isn't that what your mother tried to do? Give you rules? And all you wanted to do was break them.*

"I can't believe I was going to turn her in like some kind of criminal! How could I be so stupid?"

As soon as they'd come home from the hospital, Grace had sent Roan downstairs to take a shower and go to sleep. Even though it was hardly afternoon, she knew that Roan needed the rest. Grace figured that she should probably be doing the same thing herself, but she was just so thirsty. She just needed to have a drink.

Grace found herself staring at the refrigerator again. There was beer in the fridge. Tosh always had some around. He wouldn't miss them, Grace figured. He was probably out right now, buying some more on the boardwalk, kicking himself for being so indiscreet.

She felt like smashing her head against the wall. *Through the refrigerator door is more like it,* she told herself, *to get what's inside. Just one drink. But you can't have just one,* she told herself.

"I've had a hard day, haven't I?" Grace whispered to herself. "Maybe if I just look at it, I won't want it," she said, snatching open the door of the fridge and pulling out a cold bottle. She slid it onto the counter and stepped away. It was a twist-off. She could see that from where she stood.

"No messy appliances needed," she commented.

Before she could stop herself, she'd taken the bottle in her hands and she was trying to get a good grip on the top. But the bottle was cold and her hands were sweating, and she couldn't get the cap to turn at all.

"Damn it!" she snapped after a moment, banging the top against the counter.

"Need some help there, Grace?"

At the sound of the voice behind her, Grace snatched her hand away from the bottle as though it were on fire. She whirled, her face red and guilty. Tosh stood leaning in the doorway of the kitchen.

"What are you doing wandering around here?" Grace snapped.

"Just came back to try and explain," he sighed. "You sure you don't need a little hand there, Grace?" he asked, nodding at the beer.

"I don't need any help from you, thanks," she replied. She could feel her face burning. *Why do you care what he thinks anyway?* she asked herself. *It's none of his business.*

"Well, let me ask you a favor, all right?"

"Let's hear it first," Grace said.

"Look, you know things are shaky with Kate and me right now—"

"'Things are shaky with Kate and me'?" Grace mimicked him. "Were you upstairs? That was you, right? Things aren't shaky, pal. Things are over."

"Some things are never over, Grace," Tosh said, glancing at the unopened bottle of beer beside her. "You ought to know that."

Grace felt herself turn red.

"Grace," Tosh begged, "I need a place to stay. Please, can you let me stay here, just until I can get Kate to understand what happened. You know she's so upset right now, I can hardly talk to her."

"All of a sudden you want to talk?" Grace asked. "You didn't want to talk with that other girl."

"Some you talk to, and then," Tosh paused, "some you don't. I can't imagine you don't know what I mean."

"I *don't* think I know what you mean," Grace replied icily.

"Pour us both a drink and I'll explain it to you," he offered.

Grace shook her head. "No, thanks," she managed to squeak out.

"Hard, isn't it?" Tosh's voice was low and full of concern. "I know how it is, Grace. We all have our vices." He paused and looked at her for a long time. "Don't we?"

"You are a slime, aren't you?" Grace said. "Now that the game is up, there's no reason to pretend anymore, is that it? Remember earlier, lover-boy? Upstairs in your girlfriend's room? I was there. It doesn't bode well for you as a suitor."

"How about just as a lover?" he asked, his voice husky.

Grace could hardly believe her ears. And she definitely couldn't control her mouth. She burst into laughter.

"How about you get out, you jerk?" Grace answered.

Tosh's face turned red, and he stalked from the kitchen.

"I needed a good laugh," Grace called after him. "Thanks."

FIVE

Bo dropped the two bags he was carrying onto the ground. His backpack was pretty light, just a few T-shirts and a pair of pants inside, but the duffel he'd packed for Roan was giving him a sore neck. He'd put practically everything he could find in it. Roan had left behind most of her clothes. Somehow she'd collected quite a lot of stuff in the short time she'd been at Grace's.

Bo leaned back against the boardwalk railing, rubbing his right shoulder. He hadn't planned on carrying the duffel all day. He'd thought, for some reason, that he would be able to find Roan pretty quickly. But so far there had been no sign of her. He'd spent most of the morning on the beach, dragging the huge bag around feeling like a real dork. The beach wasn't a great place to bring luggage.

"Why don't you start building yourself a sand castle over there," some huge muscle-bound creep had yelled at him. "You could move in by the afternoon if you're lucky!"

The girls sitting nearby giggled. *And if you're lucky, the Wizard of Oz will fix his machine and give you a brain to go with that body,* Bo thought. But instead of speaking, he just smiled a tight smile, put his head down, and kept walking. That was the price you had to pay when you were outweighed by at least a hundred pounds.

The lifeguards, it turned out, weren't much help either.

"You want to know if I've seen one particular girl? I've seen so many today, I'll be counting bikinis in my sleep tonight!"

"Hey, friend, I'm a lifeguard. I save the ones who are drowning, not the ones who are running away."

After he'd walked the length of the beach twice, up and back, Bo went to the amusement park at the end of the boardwalk. Asking at the game stalls was also a disaster. It was like everyone was a closet comedian just waiting for the chance to do stand-up.

"Have I seen a pretty blonde, he wants to know?" The ring-toss guy winked at the crowd. "And if I'd seen her, he thinks I'd tell anyone else? What is he, crazy?" This uninspired skit drew appreciative laughter from the crowd.

"This town is full of pretty blondes, kid!" the guy who set up cans for the softball throw said. "Go to the beach, you'll find a hundred of them in less than ten minutes."

"You're looking for a pretty blonde. I'm looking for a pretty blonde. We're *all* looking for a pretty blonde," the roller-coaster guy sighed.

"Has she got a sister?" the guy selling hot pretzels asked.

"I don't know," Bo answered. "Why?"

"If she had a sister, I might help you look for her. But if it's just the one girl . . ." He shrugged and threw three more pretzels onto a plate covered in salt.

What was infuriating was that Bo knew he couldn't be everywhere at once. What if Roan was on the beach, now that he had come to the amusement park? What if she was playing the ring-toss and he was already down by the hoop throw? The amusement park was too big. Too crowded.

Suddenly he realized all of Ocean City was too big and too crowded. It really was easy to run away. And a lot harder to find someone.

Bo sighed and turned around to lean on the railing. The crowds on the beach were beginning to thin. Everyone knew that prime tanning hours were over. The lingerers were the swimmers, the people with sweatshirts and books, the older couples bringing picnic dinners to eat on the sand. Most of the kids his age were on their way home. But before Bo gave up on the beach and boardwalk altogether, there was still one person he should see. He wasn't looking forward to that meeting in the least.

"Better now than later," he muttered, pulling on his backpack and hoisting the duffel. Bo walked a bit farther toward the end of the boardwalk, then dropped down onto the sand.

Somehow, even though the sun was just starting to go down outside, it was always dark here. Perpetual night, Bo thought, and shivered. He walked along underneath the wooden boardwalk until he heard the sounds of conversation: a muffled swear, a low hum, the screech of a laugh. He saw the shadowy shapes floating in front of him and put the bags down in the sand.

"Billy," he called. "Is Billy in there?"

"Who wants to know?"

"I'm a friend of Roan's," he said.

"Ah, yeah," the voice said, "aren't we all."

A pale body untangled itself and came toward him. Billy, shirtless and visibly drunk.

"I'm looking for Roan," Bo said.

"Oh, yeah, I remember you. What happened?" Billy asked sarcastically. "Did she run away from you?"

"No," Bo said angrily. "Not from me."

"But you're the one who don't know where she is?"

"No," Bo shook his head, "I don't."

"Well, then, she must want it that way," Billy said, leaning back and slipping his hand into his pocket. "Don't you think?"

"Have you seen her?" Bo asked. "Is she all right?"

"I'm sure she's fine." Billy nodded. "She's fine. And with friends. And she's fine and friendly, too." Billy started laughing.

"Do you know where she is?" Bo asked, clenching his fingers into fists. "I just want to see her."

"Ha, the next time you see her, she'll be a movie star." Billy laughed. "The next time you see her, you'll be sitting in the dark theater, lonely as a baby, staring up at her on the big screen."

"What do you mean?" Bo asked. "Did she go to L.A.?" California, he thought. That was farther than he'd expected to go.

"I mean she found something better than you. So get lost. All right?" Billy picked up a broken bottle from the sand. "All right?" he said again, and then turned back to his friends and faded into the darkness.

"All right," Bo agreed. He climbed back onto the boardwalk and sat on a low green bench. He watched the people as they passed, staring at every girl—even the ones who didn't look any-thing like Roan.

It was starting to get dark, and the only other places left—police stations and hospitals—Bo couldn't bring himself to consider. He sighed and kicked the wooden railing with his sneaker, thinking for the hundredth time, *If only Grace hadn't gotten so mad last night . . .*

Bo knew why she was angry, but he didn't want to admit to himself that she had a right to be. He was sixteen. He could take care of him-self. So why did Grace have to treat him like such a baby, when she had done so much more, and worse, when she was even younger?

And why had Roan run away?

When Chelsea got home from another sketch-ing session on the beach, she was starving. She had watched too many people eating hot dogs and crab cakes, fresh clams and oysters, giant pretzels, cotton candy, and ice cream. And she'd seen too many tight bikinis and swim trunks—which had helped her from snacking herself. Until now. She was desperately hoping that someone had gone shopping. But then she re-membered that shopping was probably the last thing on everyone's mind but her own.

She was surprised to find Grace and Kate sit-ting in the living room. First, of course, because no one ever sat in the living room. And second, because they were sitting there so quietly that at first Chelsea hadn't seen them, and when she did, she'd been so surprised that she'd yelped. They each swiveled a head slowly in her direction.

"Hello?" Chelsea said tentatively.

"Hmmm," was all she got from the figures on the beige couch.

"Have either of you eaten?" Chelsea tried again, and got two head shakes and a couple of grunts.

"Are you two all right?" She walked in and stood in front of the couch.

"It hasn't been the best day, Chelsea," Kate reminded her.

"Yeah, it sure hasn't," Chelsea agreed. "But you two are hanging out in here like you're sitting *chivas*. Isn't that what David calls it?"

Grace snorted. "It's *shiva*, not *Chivas*. That's the drink."

"Oh, right. Sorry." Chelsea smiled weakly. "Anyway, you're sitting in here looking like someone died."

"Someone might," Kate said.

"I thought Marta said Dominic would be okay," Chelsea said. "Where is she, anyway?"

"She's still at the hospital," Grace said, glancing over at Kate. Kate shrugged.

"What about Roan?"

"Roan's downstairs, cleaning up her room," Kate said.

"And no, we still don't know where Bo is," Grace added.

"I'm sorry," Chelsea offered.

"I know," Grace replied stiffly. "So am I."

"So you've been out sketching?" Kate asked.

"Yep. I have to start on the ad campaign tomorrow night, and I want to be ready."

"On a Sunday night?" Grace asked. "That's odd, isn't it?"

"I guess so." Chelsea shrugged. "Paul's rented out a condo for us to use as an office—"

"A condo. How . . . convenient." Grace smirked.

Chelsea laughed. "No, it's not like it sounds. I told you, Grace, we've been through that. The office is for me and the copywriter he's hired. Since we both sort of have day jobs, we'll be meeting in the evenings."

"Sounds like you'll be working long days," Kate said.

"Long days and longer nights," Grace added.

"Oh, come on." Chelsea blushed. "What do you think we'll be doing?"

"The question is, what do *you* think you'll be doing?" Grace asked.

"Trying to sell seafood, I guess," Chelsea replied. "Besides, I don't even know the copywriter."

"That's a good point," Kate agreed. "You're going to go spend all your nights in a condo with a guy you've never met before."

"All right." Chelsea laughed. "It's an unusual work arrangement, but it's still work. You think I can't work with a man professionally just because there's going to be a bed nearby?"

"Let's just hope this copywriter is as professional as you are," Grace warned.

"I've never done any creative work like this before," Chelsea admitted. "I hope it works out. I've always thought it would be hard to find someone to collaborate with artistically."

"It's hard to find someone to 'collaborate' with in any sense," Kate said cynically.

"Yeah," Chelsea agreed. "I guess neither of us has had the best luck with men this year."

"You can say that again," Kate said.

"I never would have expected it from him," Chelsea continued. "And definitely not in your own room. How rude!"

"Mmm, my own— What? Oh, *Tosh*. Right. Rude is a polite way to put it," Kate said, shaking her head. "What a mistake, huh?"

"Of course Tosh," Chelsea said. "Did you have another boyfriend earlier today that I didn't know about?"

"No, unfortunately he was the only one," Kate admitted.

Chelsea was about to ask her what she meant when her stomach made a noise so loud that they all had to stare at it.

"Hungry?" Grace asked.

"Maybe just a little," Chelsea admitted.

"There is a kitchen in this house." Grace smiled.

"Oh?" Chelsea asked in mock surprise. "Is that what that room is? And am I supposed to . . . I don't know . . . *cook*? Food? For myself?"

Her stomach growled again.

"You'd better do something," Kate said.

Chelsea laughed and walked away. The front door opened just as she turned into the kitchen.

"Hey, Bo," she said as she passed him, wondering what kind of dinner she might be able to find that wouldn't include canned tuna or bean dip. Suddenly she stopped and whirled around.

"Bo!" she screamed. Kate and Grace leapt from the couch.

Grace rushed over to him, her arms out. "Where have you been?" she cried. Bo let her take him in her arms, but when he didn't hug her back, Grace dropped her hands and stepped away.

"Are you okay?" she asked tentatively, biting her lip.

Bo nodded.

"I was worried about you," Grace said.

"I know," he replied softly. "I'm sorry."

He looked around at them, and glanced at Grace once. "Listen, I need some help," he said, his voice small. "I've been looking all day and I can't find her."

"Roan?" Grace asked. "She's here."

Bo's face lit up, and finally he looked Grace in the eye. "She's here?"

"She called Grace for help," Kate explained.

"We had to go get her at the hospital," Chelsea blurted out.

"At the hospital?" Bo's face went white as a sheet.

"She's okay," Kate said, stepping forward and turning Bo toward the stairs. "In fact, she's down in her room now. I'm sure she'd be really glad to see you."

Bo nodded. They watched him walk down the stairs. Then they heard the soft tap on Roan's door, which opened and closed without a word from either Bo or Roan.

Grace stood still, gazing down the stairwell.

"He came home, Grace," Chelsea said.

"Hmmm." Grace nodded.

"He came to you for help," Kate added.

"Maybe," Grace sighed.

"Let him go one step at a time," Kate said.

"He can't stay mad forever," Chelsea offered.

Grace nodded, her eyes bright with tears. "I know," she whispered. "But sometimes it's hard to wait."

Bo could hardly believe that this Roan was the same girl he'd been out with the night before. Her white-blond hair wasn't teased, and she wasn't wearing any makeup. She didn't look like a girl who spent her evenings partying with a bottle of booze and a pack of cigarettes.

She looked clean and fresh. And she was still as beautiful, that was for sure.

Bo sat on the edge of her bed, watching Roan as she leaned against the wall with her knees up.

"I spent all day looking for you," Bo said. He was trying not to sound accusatory, but his voice sounded sharp, even to himself. "I was worried," he added.

Roan looked over at him and smiled. "I'm sorry."

"You don't have to apologize," he said quickly. "Where did you go?"

"I went to see Billy, to see if he knew anyplace to go."

"Yeah," Bo said. "I saw him today. Just before I came home. I knew he'd seen you, but he wouldn't tell me anything. Except that you were going to be a movie star—whatever that meant."

Roan looked up. "He said that?" Her eyebrows drew together, and an angry expression came over her face. "He *knew*," she whispered to herself. "I can't believe it."

"Can't believe what?" Bo asked.

"I thought he was my friend, that's all." Roan shrugged. "He sent me to some guy's house. He said the guy was cool. That I could crash there for a few days." Roan sighed. "But the guy was a real nightmare." She laughed and ran a hand through her hair. "Yeah, he wanted to make me a movie star, all right. But not the kind of movies you can go see if you're under eighteen."

"Are you kidding?" Bo asked. "You mean . . . he wanted—"

"Don't say it. Please," Roan begged. "It makes me sick just thinking about it."

"Well, what happened?"

"I jumped out the bathroom window, ran to the bus station, and bought a ticket," Roan said.

"You were going to leave?" Bo asked sharply. "Just like that?"

"Not because I wanted to," Roan said quickly. "I just—I just didn't know what else to do."

"So why didn't you go?" Bo asked bitterly.

"Because this guy showed up with a knife, tried to kill me, and stabbed Dominic instead," Roan rattled off. "It was kind of distracting. I missed the bus. And besides, the guy tore up my ticket anyway."

Bo looked away. He felt angry and hurt that she would have left without saying anything to him. "Well, I'm sorry I wasn't there to help," he said tightly.

"I'm not," Roan answered softly.

Bo looked up sharply.

"Otherwise," she said, "instead of Dominic—it might have been you."

Bo blushed and turned away. "Come on," he said. "You wouldn't have cared that much."

Roan leaned over and touched his hand. "Of course I would have," she said. "I didn't want to leave. I was just . . . afraid."

She reached for a bottle of soda on her night table. Her hand was shaking pretty badly.

"Can I have a sip of that too?" Bo asked, his throat suddenly dry.

Roan nodded, but before she could pass it to him, he stood up and walked over to the table.

His hand brushed hers when she gave him the bottle, and immediately he started to sweat. He wanted to tell her how worried he'd been about her. He wanted to tell her all the things he'd thought about during the day. He took a deep breath. But when he looked up, he could see that she was crying.

"Are you okay?" he asked, setting down the

soda and reaching out to put his hand softly on hers. She turned her palm up and their fingers laced together. She was holding his hand so tightly that it hurt.

"Roan," he whispered. "It's okay. I'm glad you're all right. I was really worried."

She nodded, but the tears kept coming down.

"Do you want me to sit next to you?" Bo asked, his throat dry again.

Roan nodded as Bo sat on the bed. He put his arm around her, and she leaned against him and started sobbing.

"Okay, okay," Bo whispered, touching her hair. Roan cried for a few moments, and then she started hiccuping. Bo rubbed her back lightly until she caught her breath.

"I'm so glad Grace was here," Roan sniffed into his shirt.

"You are?" Bo asked, surprised.

"She came to help me, and she told off the cops and everything."

"She did?" Bo said, smiling. "Yeah, she's pretty good at telling people off."

"'Couldn't you let her go to the bathroom to wash up?'" Roan's voice came out sharp and hard, and she sounded so much like his sister that Bo jerked his head back to look at her. Roan continued, "'She's not a thief!' 'Of course not, Miss Caywood.'"

Bo started chuckling, picturing the scene so well. A few policemen were no match for Grace.

"Yeah, she's okay," Bo agreed. "When you're on her side, that is," he added seriously.

Roan nodded. "But her side is a pretty cool place to be," she said softly.

SIX

It was late, and Marta was eating the dinner that the nurse had brought her. It was gross, and every disgusting bite reminded her of being back in her own hospital bed, the food sticking in her throat.

A weak moan from the bed startled her from her thoughts. She wheeled closer to see Dominic's eyelids fluttering. She reached for the call button. Then her hand froze. She just didn't want to press it yet.

She watched Dominic's eyes open slowly. They took a moment to focus. Marta knew what he was seeing: white, white, and more white. A cracked ceiling, a TV in the upper corner above the door. Then there would be the remembering. Bit by bit. The corridor, and then further back. The emergency room and then further back. The ambulance. And then all the way back to the bus station. Buying a ticket. Going to the bathroom. The commotion and screaming. Opening the door and the blond girl running into him. And then someone else, his head turning, the flash of the knife.

When he flinched, Marta flinched with him, knowing exactly where he was in his mind. The terrifying moment of clear memory. The moment of confusion. A moment that might replay itself a hundred times. A thousand times. In her case, perhaps a million times or more.

Finally he turned his head and saw her there, and Marta no longer knew what he was thinking.

"Do you know where you are?" she asked.

He nodded.

"Do you remember why you're here?"

"Stabbed." His voice came out as a breath.

Marta nodded back at him. "The doctors said you'll be fine."

"It doesn't feel much like that."

"No, it probably doesn't."

"Why are you here?" he asked her.

Marta had been wondering that herself.

"You don't have to answer," he said, seeing her distress. "It doesn't matter."

"I'm here because I know you," she said finally. "And I can't let people I know lie in hospitals alone. I've experienced it, remember? It isn't very fun."

"I remember," Dominic said, coughing lightly. "I remember every minute."

"You can't stay here, of course," Marta went on. "You know that. As soon as you're well enough to leave, you should. Otherwise they'll start charging you an arm and a leg—"

"How about just a pint of blood?" Dominic interrupted, referring to his short-lived career as Dracula at Horror Hall on the boardwalk. "I'm pretty good at getting those."

"This is no time to joke," Marta snapped.

"Why not?"

Marta shook her head and shrugged. "Do what you like, I guess. If you think it's funny."

"I guess I don't think it's funny," Dominic replied softly.

"You don't have anywhere to go," Marta said, finally spilling out what she'd been thinking about for most of the day. "And I know you don't know anyone here."

"Mr. DiPaolo," he whispered. "I know him."

"Right." Marta laughed. "He'd be a great nurse. And while he's off getting in imaginary accidents, where will you be? Nowhere. That's what I'm saying. In a day or so, when you can be moved, you'll come to my house. I'll take care of you until you get better."

Dominic raised his eyebrows and studied her.

"Why do you want to do that?" he finally asked.

"Because," Marta sighed. "Because I'd do it for anyone else I knew. You'll leave when you get better, anyway. I'm offering you a place to stay. That's all. This doesn't change anything between us."

"You don't have to do this," Dominic said.

"I know," Marta responded. "But there's a reason I don't let people lie on the street bleeding. It has to do with me, not who those people are. I won't make an exception of you, Dominic."

Marta pushed back from the bed a little and let her hands linger on the wheels of her chair. She sat straight and quiet. Dominic lifted his head from the pillow and looked at her for a long time. She tried to meet his gaze, but found she couldn't.

"I thought I saw you earlier," Dominic said finally, dropping his head back against the pillow. His voice was hoarse and soft. "Isn't that strange? I thought I saw your face pass by me."

"You may have," she said carefully. "I was at the clinic when they brought you in."

"Was it hard?" he asked, his eyes solid black knots of pain.

"Was what hard?" Marta answered.

He looked deep into her eyes before he said, "Watching them save me."

The covers were getting in her way. For that matter, so were the pillows. And the sheets and the mattress. Kate sighed and sat up in bed. *Give up already,* she said to herself. *There's no way you're sleeping tonight, Kate Quinn.*

She reached over and turned on her bedside lamp, fluffed her pillows, and picked up the book she'd been reading. She found her place and prepared to settle in for a long read.

The book was a history of Greenpeace, the environmentalist organization. Her job last summer as an assistant for Dr. Shelby Haynes at the Safe Seas Foundation had piqued her interest in marine life, not to mention the "green" politics of the environmental movement. Greenpeace had always been a group that Kate admired. It was the kind of activism she would want to do, if she ever found herself more active than lying in bed listlessly reading a book, that is.

When she realized that she'd read the same paragraph eight or nine times and still had no idea what it said, she put the book down. Right now painting seals, dodging harpoons, and speeding around in motorized life rafts wasn't as absorbing as it might have been. Particularly in bed. And alone.

Kate sighed and squeezed her eyes shut, trying not to cry again. This wasn't like her, to be feeling so lonely and small. She was independent. And careful. And goal oriented. An achiever. Right?

Keep saying it, Kate thought. *Someone might believe you.*

Right now all Kate felt like was a lonely woman awake at night in her bedroom. *How could I have been so blind?* She'd have liked to pretend it didn't matter to her, but of course it did. She'd thought Tosh had cared for her.

Kate sighed. She just didn't understand how, after thinking through everything so clearly, after weighing and considering, after making all the right choices, she could end up so wrong. And so lonely. And afraid that she had lost something much more precious and important than she could afford: Justin.

Thinking of him made Kate feel guilty. Considering what happened with Tosh today. Considering that Kate was just lying in bed being angry about it. She was embarrassed at how quickly her mind could turn to thoughts of Justin. But she just couldn't help wondering if Tosh wasn't the first mistake she'd made.

Wasn't it the romantics who were supposed

to get hurt? Well, Kate definitely hadn't been a romantic.

Perhaps that was her problem. Perhaps she should have let her heart make her decisions, not her head.

Justin had been back in Ocean City only six days, so falling into a settled routine wasn't going to happen overnight. Not after almost drowning in a storm in the Caribbean, and then having to spend two grueling months on a Portuguese fishing boat where no one spoke any English. It was the kind of life experience that might account for trouble sleeping.

That, and also returning home to find the girl you loved shacked up with someone else.

Justin growled and punched his pillow a few times, telling himself he just wanted to make it more comfortable. It wasn't as though Connor's couch could be mistaken for luxury accommodations of any kind. And since it looked as though he wouldn't be getting any sleep, he could at least try not getting a stiff neck, as well.

Justin rolled over and let his head drop off the side of the couch. His watch was lying on the floor next to him. The hands glowed up at him accusingly. He sighed and sat up in the darkness. Maybe a swim would help him relax. That's what he usually did when he had trouble sleeping.

The last time he'd gone out to the ocean at night, Kate had been there too. She'd really made him crazy then. He knew how much he'd missed her. He had thought of her every day and night that he was gone. But still, it had surprised him how badly he'd wanted her. How good it had felt to hold her again.

But she had definitely put out that fire. Loudly and clearly. And without much remorse, it had seemed to Justin. So she'd found someone new, and Justin was only a memory for her. We need to move on, she'd said, or some garbage like that. Well, okay, he'd done it.

So that made two Kates he'd lost. The woman and his little boat. Not a very good record.

"Must've been the name," Justin muttered.

In Justin and Kate's relationship, it had always been his boat that had come between them. He needed to sail away to be free, and she wanted him to stay and give up the ocean. It seemed pretty ironic, after all of that, that *Kate* the boat was the first one to go.

Justin stood in the darkness and walked to the tiny balcony. He stepped out into the night air and tilted his head, listening to the sound of the waves. How different the sound was when you listened to it while standing on a steady little balcony, as opposed to hearing and feeling the waves at the same time, lying on your back on the deck of a boat.

Suddenly Justin was filled with nostalgia. He already missed the sea. Even though he'd come so close to dying, he'd had an incredible time sailing across the ocean. The trip had been everything he'd imagined it could be.

Well, it had been almost everything, Justin reminded himself. There was a time when he thought he'd have his boat, and the real Kate to accompany him.

Justin wondered where the boat was now, or what was left of her, anyway. He heard a whimpering behind him and turned to find Mooch sitting in the doorway.

"Wondering what's wrong with me, huh, boy?" Justin leaned down and gave the dog a hug. "Wondering what we're gonna do now?" Justin scratched the dog behind the ears until his tail started slapping the floor.

"That's right," he said to Mooch. "Good idea, buddy. Let's find our boat and move on. Stop living in the past."

Justin was getting on with his life, just as Kate said he should. Marta was a smart and beautiful woman. And strong, as well. She could understand a relationship for what it was, without attaching all kinds of expectations and demands. If the way she sped around in her wheelchair was any indication, she was a woman intent on moving forward.

But remember, a voice suddenly reminded him, *you are alone right now. Because whatever Marta might say, and however tough and strong she looks and acts, the fact is that she isn't with you. She's at the hospital. At someone else's bedside.*

SEVEN

"That's not the way she looks! Her eyebrows *don't* meet in the middle like that!" the woman screeched, sticking her hand over Chelsea's shoulder and smudging the charcoal line Chelsea had just drawn.

"And her hair is *shiny*. Can't you make it shiny?"

Chelsea bit her lip, choking back the words that were on the tip of her tongue.

"It's a bit hard to do 'shiny' in black and white," she said through gritted teeth.

The woman snorted.

Chelsea was trying to do a portrait on the boardwalk; part of The Face Place's new "expanded" services. Her boss called it a promotion. Chelsea was now the official Roving Portraitist. The bonus was being in the sunshine.

The drawback was that there was enough room outside of the small Face Place storefront for the lucky model's whole family to stand behind her and criticize everything she did.

At the moment Chelsea was doing what was supposed to have been an inexpensive "Quick Charcoal Sketch" of a dark-haired twelve-year-old. A few lines here and there, the suggestion of the face, something interesting and impressionistic. Or at least that was how she thought it would be. But that was the ninth or tenth time the girl's mother had touched her work, and Chelsea was on the verge of screaming.

If she smudges it again, Chelsea thought, *I'll poke her in the eye with my pencil. Make that both eyes. And ears. And nose.*

"That's not quite her chin, is it?" the mother said, leaning over. She was about to put her finger to the paper again when her husband grabbed her by the shoulder.

"Why don't you give her a chance to draw it herself," he said. "That's what we're paying for, now, isn't it?"

By the time she was finished, Chelsea had turned a rather ordinary little girl into a mature-looking, beautiful young woman. Straighter nose. Daintier chin. Thinner eyebrows. Jutting cheekbones.

"It's perfect," the mother said when Chelsea

gave it to her. "It's a perfect likeness, isn't it?" she asked her husband, holding the portrait out and turning to him.

"Do I really look like that?" the little girl asked skeptically.

"Of course you do," her mother said. "This woman is a trained artist.. She only draws what she sees."

Then be happy I'm not drawing you, Chelsea thought. *Otherwise you'd get a nice charcoal picture of a bulldozer.*

The father agreed, smiling generously, and handed Chelsea a tip that almost made up for it. Almost.

"Boy," Chelsea muttered to herself after they'd gone, "I'm glad I'm not going to have to make my living as a street artist. What agony."

"What agony is right," a familiar voice said behind her. "Out on the boardwalk in the sun . . . What are you complaining about?"

Chelsea turned to find Grace laughing at her from behind a very chic pair of sunglasses. Grace's hair was pulled up and back into a stylish chignon. She was wearing a deep-taupe skirt and jacket. At first glance Chelsea thought it was rather conservative for Grace, but then she saw the silk piping and striking cut. Chelsea whistled.

"You look fantastic," she said. "But don't tell me you pound the sand in that getup. That's a little too fine for beach stands, Grace."

"I know," Grace agreed. "I don't usually do the beach like this, but this morning I had to make an exception. I'm actually going to see someone."

"Not David?" Chelsea asked. "In that outfit, your date must be a millionaire."

"Oh, it's not a 'date' someone. It's a business someone," Grace corrected.

Chelsea raised her eyebrows and nodded. *Some business,* she thought.

"What are you doing, Grace? Buying the Ocean City Grand Hotel?"

"Not quite," Grace replied. "Maybe that will be my *next* project. For now, though, I'll take one at a time. Speaking of business, how's the art world?" Grace asked, looking at the charcoal debris collecting at Chelsea's feet. "Should I start scouting real estate for a gallery? One with a shower stall?"

"What?"

"You're covered with black smudges." Grace laughed. "When people say artists get into their work, they aren't kidding. What did you do? Climb into your charcoal box?"

Chelsea blushed. "Well, not exactly. But I kind of lose track of myself when I work. Forget what I'm wiping my hands on, sometimes. I've ruined a lot of nice clothes that way."

"It's not just on your clothes." Grace smiled.

"Where else?" Chelsea asked nervously.

"Your right ear."

"Okay," Chelsea admitted, "that's not a usual spot. But I felt like tearing my hair out just now. Maybe I got closer than I thought. Anyway, no one cares what I look like, as long as I draw more than one eyebrow."

"You mean your portrait wasn't exactly accurate?" Grace chuckled.

"You said it. Now that I have a real job to go to tonight, I'm finding it pretty hard to stand in the sun and sweat over some tourist's dream of having a daughter who looks like Julia Roberts."

"I'm finding it pretty hard to stand in the sun and sweat for any reason lately." Grace laughed, looking around them.

"Yeah," Chelsea agreed. "The second summer around, I'm beginning to feel the difference between coming here for a day on the beach and living here. I thought I'd never get tired of working outside."

"Now you know how I feel about this place," Grace said. "I've lived here my whole life."

"I'm beginning to understand," Chelsea said.

"Well, I've got to go," Grace said, checking her watch. "Good luck."

"You too," Chelsea said. She watched as Grace made her way through the crowd on the boardwalk. In that outfit, she really stood out from the crowd of bikinis and bathing suits. Chelsea laughed as she saw people stepping back out of Grace's way. *I wouldn't stand in her way either,* Chelsea said to herself.

Time for some refreshment. Chelsea gazed at the stalls nearby. Italian ices, Good Humor bars, frozen daiquiris. There was too long a line at the banana-shake van, so Chelsea strolled over to the ice-cream shop.

Chelsea gazed longingly at all the flavors. Mocha Almond Fudge? Pistachio Ripple? Pralines and Cream? She never was good at making these kinds of decisions.

"A single dip of Strawberries and Cream, please," a deep voice said from her left.

Chelsea turned to find herself looking at a man she would share strawberries and cream with for the rest of her life. If only he'd ask. She still had her mouth open, staring at the empty space he'd left, when the woman behind the counter finally caught her attention.

"Something for you, dear?" she asked with a knowing smile.

"I doubt you sell it," Chelsea replied. "So I'll have one of whatever he had."

"You and everyone after you, I imagine," the woman replied. Chelsea turned to find three women standing in line behind her, all heads turned to the doorway.

Chelsea shrugged. "I had my moment, though, didn't I?" she asked as she took the ice cream and gave the woman her money.

"You sure did, dear."

Chelsea left the shop and walked back to her small portable easel. She sat on a bench and settled in to watch the beachgoers.

She thought about the hard time she'd had with the family this morning. It had only been a few days ago that Paul Hagen offered her work on his ad campaign, but ever since then she'd found it hard to enjoy the portrait sketching like she used to. Once more, Chelsea had a brief, troubling thought about her unknown partner. Paul had said that he was great, that he had a unique and witty sense of humor. Chelsea just hoped that he was easy to work with. This was a once-in-a-lifetime job opportunity. Nowhere else in the world besides Ocean City would she get a job offer like this. Definitely not back in New York.

"This is one project I'm really going to follow through with," she said to herself. "I'm going to follow it all the way to happiness." *Or at least to a few free meals at the restaurant we're doing the ads for,* she mused.

Chelsea smiled and caught up with a glob of Strawberries and Cream that had trailed down the cone to her fingers and skipped along her wrist, and was steadily winding its way down to her elbow.

She began to watch the pattern of strange bodies that passed. She almost felt like she was watching TV. She saw three bathing suits she wanted, a new hairstyle, a great pair of sandals, and seven or eight funky kinds of sunglasses. There were so many interesting people in this place. And so many baseball caps. Chelsea was sure she had learned more about sports teams in her time at Ocean City than she had in her entire life.

After fifteen minutes of careful study, everyone started to look alike. Until she found herself staring at a face that didn't seem to fit in with the rest. A very familiar face, actually. Red hair and freckles.

Connor Riordan was walking toward her in the crowd, his eyes roving and darting.

Maybe he won't see me, Chelsea thought. But she couldn't seem to look away. Finally their eyes met. Chelsea watched the flicker of recognition cross Connor's face. Then there was a moment of—what? Fear? Indecision? Just as Chelsea thought he would try to walk past without saying anything at all, he smiled and came over to her.

"So," he said, his Irish accent drawing the word out.

"Connor."

Chelsea was surprised at how weak her voice sounded. Her lips had trouble with his name, as though it were an awkward sound in her mouth.

"This is a surprise, eh?" Connor said, nodding his head at the crowd and gazing around.

"Not really," Chelsea replied carefully. "Ocean City isn't that big. It's bound to happen every once in a while."

"Eating ice cream again, I see," Connor said, pointing to the dripping cone. "You don't plan on throwing it at anyone today, do ya?"

Chelsea knew Connor was referring to the last time they'd seen each other on the board-walk. Chelsea had seen Connor walking and laughing with another girl; she'd been so mad that she'd thrown her ice cream down in a rage. Luckily for the girl Connor was with, she'd managed to throw it on an Immigration officer, who hadn't noticed when Connor and the girl ran off down an alley. It had turned out that she was a recent arrival from Ireland, and Chelsea had helped her escape.

"I don't know," Chelsea shot back. "Not unless you plan on escorting illegal aliens around town."

"You mean *female* illegal aliens, of course," Connor said.

Chelsea shrugged. "I don't mean anything," she replied. "You're a free man, aren't you? Isn't that what we decided?"

Connor sighed and turned away from her. "Is it, now? I guess that's right if you say so."

What did he mean by that? Seeing other people *was* his idea. Was he suggesting that he didn't want to do that?

"So you're working?" Connor asked softly.

"What does it look like?"

"Looks like you're eating ice cream, which is melting by the by if you don't mind my saying." He shrugged. "Never can tell with you artists," he said lightly. "Could be drawing. Could be drawing and getting paid for it."

"Are you saying you don't think I deserve to be paid for my work?" Chelsea demanded.

"Not at all," Connor replied. "Only, sometimes it's hard to tell the difference between working for yourself and working for someone else."

"And I only know about working for myself, is that it?" Chelsea snapped. "While you, of course, know all there is to know about getting paid by someone else."

"Maybe," Connor said defensively.

"Watch out!" a voice screamed.

Connor and Chelsea turned to find a trio of speeding Rollerbladers bearing down on them. They leapt away as the Rollerbladers, dressed in black and neon green and yellow, whizzed by them.

"Someone should ticket them!" Connor exclaimed. "Practically killing innocent people," he muttered.

Chelsea sighed, secretly glad for the interruption.

"Connor, look. If it's only snide comments you have to offer, then I guess we still don't have much to say to each other," she said bluntly, fighting back tears.

Connor groaned and ran a hand through his fiery hair.

"Look, I don't mean to snipe," he said impatiently. He turned away and stepped over to the railing, looking out over the beach. "But I can't even joke with you anymore. You've made it very clear that you don't appreciate my sense of humor."

"I do appreciate your sense of humor, but as your only positive attribute, it becomes a little tiresome," Chelsea replied, throwing the sticky napkin she held into a garbage can.

"Oh, does it?" Connor choked out, whirling around. "You think that's tiresome? I'll tell you what's tiresome. Watching the clutter you left behind grow and grow and grow. It was tiresome to watch you go from one unfinished thing to another. But even though I couldn't find my clothes to get dressed in, it never slowed you down. You just kept on your merry way, happy to take money from your parents."

Chelsea's jaw dropped. "What do you mean I was happy to take money from them?" she said. "I hated taking money from them. But *we* didn't have any. *We* weren't making any—"

"I was making some!" Connor cried.

"But not enough," Chelsea said, exasperated. "They offered help and I took it. What's wrong with that? They are my parents. That's what parents are for, Connor. To help and take care of you."

Connor nodded and dropped his head. He turned back to the ocean.

"So if that's what your parents were for," he asked softly, "where did I fit in?" He faced her. "You weren't asking me to take care of you. You left me out of everything! How secure is that supposed to make me feel? The only thing I had left was my sense of humor," he said angrily. "Even *I* couldn't keep myself laughing."

"Don't try and tell me this is my fault," Chelsea shrieked. "This isn't about you feeling left out. This is about you feeling badly because you couldn't get a decent job in New York and your stubborn Irish pride couldn't stand that we were getting money from *my* parents. Go ahead and say I went from one thing to another. What about you?"

Chelsea lifted her easel into her arms as if it could protect her.

"Talk yourself up a bit, why don't you?" she went on. "What kind of a job have you got now? At least I've found a way to use my talents."

"Journalism has nothing to do with writing? Working on the paper isn't using my talents?" Connor asked.

"Not with those silly articles I read: 'Ten Terrific Tanning Tips'? That was a real investigative piece," Chelsea said.

"Oh, I see," Connor snapped back. "And a ten-dollar fake portrait is so much more worthy, right? You're no sellout. Not you."

"No, I'm not," Chelsea cried. "At least I get to draw. And I have an even better job than this now. At least I'm not working some deep fryer. That is one of your 'skills,' isn't it?"

"Oh, yeah?" Connor said smugly. Then he took a step back and bowed deeply. "Make fun if you want," he said when he straightened up. "All I needed was some room to *breathe*. And for your information," he called over his shoulder as he walked away, "I'm going to have a career after all."

Chelsea watched as his red hair disappeared down the boardwalk. Then she stumbled back and sat down on the bench, still clutching her easel to her chest.

Where did all that come from? she asked herself. *How did it get so mean so quickly?*

Chelsea felt the sun bearing down on her. She heard the laughing and screaming of a volleyball game on the beach behind her. The noise of radios tuned in to three or four different stations. She saw the hundreds of people passing in front of her on the boardwalk. So how, with all of the noise and all of the people, could she feel so alone?

Grace took a deep breath and stepped onto the porch of the small Victorian house. The house was well taken care of, freshly painted and renovated. Someone had been careful about preserving all the old and delicate details. There was a doorbell over a brass nameplate that read simply:

GENEVIEVE GUGERTY
ATTORNEY AT LAW

Grace had never expected to see the prim, businesslike woman again. The last time Grace had met with her mother's lawyer, it had been to sign papers after Ellen Caywood's death. Naturally, Grace hadn't been in the best frame of mind then.

"I hope you won't mind being bothered on a

Sunday," Grace whispered. "I have something really important to ask you about. And please," Grace said, crossing the fingers of her left hand behind her back as she reached out with her right to ring the bell. "Please don't remember what a bitch I was the last time you saw me."

EIGHT

"You look amazing!" David Jacobs exclaimed as Grace stepped out onto the deck that ran all the way around his little bungalow.

"I hope you don't expect to look that good all afternoon," David said, winking at her and planting a deep kiss on her mouth.

"Why not?" Grace asked when they came up for air.

"Because, while this outfit is a particularly stunning one, I had another suit in mind for you today."

"Another business suit?" Grace asked innocently. "How nice!"

"Well," David admitted, "it's for a certain kind of business, but not whatever you did this morning. I was thinking of something quite a bit more casual. More natural. More unrestrained."

Grace laughed. "Well, describe it to me later in detail. I'm sure I still have some negotiating left in me."

"So?" David asked. "Are you going to tell me? What have you been up to? You have that look about you. That look that says 'Watch out, I've done something!'"

"I went to see your friend, Gen," Grace said.

"Gen Gugerty? The lawyer?" David asked. "You didn't like her much, if I remember."

"I think she thought that too," Grace admitted. "Certainly I was the last person she ever expected at her door. But I think she forgave me. Extenuating circumstances and all that."

David raised an eyebrow.

"Gen gave me the language," Grace admitted.

"So what did you want to see her about?" David asked, his eyes sparkling with curiosity. "Joint tax returns? Prenuptial agreements?"

"Sorry to disappoint you," Grace explained, "but not quite along those lines. Extending the family is the mission, but not where you're concerned."

"Okay, then spill it," David urged. "Now I'm really curious."

Grace took a deep breath. "It's about Roan. I know things were getting out of control with her and Bo. You were right about that."

David shrugged. "But?"

"But I didn't handle it right," Grace said. "I

94

came down too hard. It was a power thing, and I was jealous. Worried about Bo, yes. But probably jealous, too. And you may not know this about me, but I'm a real terror when I'm jealous," Grace said, adding a little warning note to her voice.

"I see." David laughed. "I'll remember that."

"Anyway," Grace went on, "it wasn't nice. I scared the hell out of her, and look what happened. I brought her home because I wanted to help her. But that's not the way to do it."

Grace paused to try to gauge David's reaction. He was leaning back on the deck railing. He was watching her carefully, but his face was a blank. Just like him, of course, to let her get it all on the table before he commented. No good facial tics to indicate anything. He would be a great poker player. Grace breathed deeply to calm herself. The warm salty air relaxed her.

"I'm not saying she's an angel," Grace admitted, gazing down the beach. "She's definitely not. But she needs some help. And it can't be charity. It can't be some all-grown-up old offender, like me, who offers a place to stay as long as she's good. Because it's not a real home. Because I can still kick her out anytime I feel like it. And I almost did. She needs a place where she can be good *and* still make mistakes. That's a real home. That's the kind of home everyone needs."

Grace looked at David again and saw him smiling.

"Am I getting preachy? Too emotional?" she asked, a bit embarrassed.

"No," he said, "you're making a case. And now, I imagine, you're getting to the point."

"Okay," Grace blurted out, "it comes down to this. If I'm going to help her, I have to show her that I mean it. That I'm in for the long haul. I asked Gen about getting legal custody of Roan until she's old enough to take care of herself."

"I see," David said.

Grace began to pace back and forth along the deck. That wasn't much of a reaction, she thought. Was "I see" good or bad?

"Gen said that the only way to do it is to get her mother to legally appoint me as Roan's guardian." She stopped at the far end of the deck.

"Hmm."

Grace whirled at the sound and moved toward him.

"I know it, I know it," she rushed on, waving her hand to quiet any objections David might make. "I'm barely responsible enough to take care of myself. I'm already the legal guardian of another sixteen-year-old, who I at least have the benefit of being related to, and that isn't going particularly well at the moment. So okay," Grace said, finally pausing for a moment. "Now you can tell me why that's the worst idea you ever heard."

David was silent for a while. He cocked his head and stared at her until she started to fidget.

"Do I have to?" he finally asked.

"Have to what?" Grace asked nervously.

"Tell you it's the worst idea I ever heard?"

"You mean, you don't think it is?" Grace couldn't believe it. Was this the same man who'd warned her to be careful? Who'd told her not to trust Roan?

"Really?" Grace asked again.

David nodded.

"I can't believe I'm really going to do this," Grace whispered, suddenly faint. "I feel sick. I was sure you'd give me a hundred reasons not to do it."

"Of course you're afraid," David said, taking her in his arms. "You're going to do something hard. And something that already means a lot to you."

"Can you really see that?" Grace asked into his shoulder, soothed by the familiar smell of his clothes and the strength of his comforting arms.

"That's the reason I don't think it's such a bad idea," he replied. "I know you, remember. When you set your mind to something, woe be the man or beast that gets in your way."

"Well, I don't want to say anything to Roan

yet," Grace cautioned. "At least not about the custody thing. I don't want her to get her hopes up. Just in case this particular man or beast doesn't know what woe is."

"If they don't," David said, laughing, "they will when you get through with them."

Justin was on his way out for a late-morning run when he opened the door to his apartment and found Bo standing outside.

"Hey, Justin," Bo said, popping his skateboard into his hand. "How's it going?"

"Fine. How're things with you?"

"Good, good." Bo nodded. "Things are good. Crazy couple of days, though, huh? Yeah, things are all right. I was just coming over to see you."

"Oh, yeah?" Justin laughed. "For how long?"

"What do you mean?"

"How long have you been standing outside my door?"

"A few minutes," Bo said.

"Do you want to come in?" Justin asked, stepping back. *There goes the run,* he thought.

Bo moved by him and went into the tiny apartment. He walked around the living room, poked his head into Connor's bedroom, into the bathroom, into the kitchen.

"So this is it, huh?" Bo asked, staring around. "Where do you sleep?"

Justin pointed to the couch, the pile of bedding that hadn't gotten much use the night before wadded up at one end.

"Hey, Mooch," Bo said to the hairy mound piled next to the bedding, looking suspiciously doglike and alive. Mooch lifted his head, stuck his tongue out, and panted a few times in greeting. Then he yawned and dropped his big head back into Justin's blankets.

"Looks comfortable," Bo said. Justin eyed him with suspicion.

"Nice view," Bo said, sticking his head out and looking at the tiny balcony. "You can almost see the ocean."

"Mmm-hmm." Justin nodded slowly.

"And the rent's not bad, with the two of you, that is," Bo went on. "So it's pretty cool, I guess."

"Bo?" Justin interrupted.

"Yeah?"

"What do you want?"

Bo smiled innocently. "Just wanted to hang out, that's all. Talk about this and that. I was wondering how you are."

"Have a seat," Justin said. "Want a drink?"

"What have you got?"

"Water."

"No beer?"

"Bo, it's ten in the morning," Justin said, raising his eyebrow.

"Right," Bo said. "Too early, I guess. I just thought we could share one, that's all. You know, man to man."

"Man to man?" Justin asked.

"Water's fine," Bo said.

Justin went into the kitchen shaking his head. Something was definitely up with Bo. Marta had told him about the blowup he and Grace had had right before Roan took off. This was bound to be a serious conversation, the way Bo was nervously bouncing off the walls. Justin filled two glasses with water and headed back to the living room.

"Thanks," Bo said, accepting the glass Justin offered. He took a sip and put the glass down on the wobbly coffee table.

"Okay," Justin said, falling into the chair. "Are you in trouble?"

"Who, me?" Bo asked, surprised. "No way, man." He shook his head. "I'm cool."

"Okay." Justin nodded. He watched Bo carefully. Bo sat on the couch, smiling, tapping his foot on the floor, looking around aimlessly, scratching Mooch behind the ears. Patience had never been Justin's strong suit. He cracked after two full minutes of silence.

"So?" he asked pointedly.

"So," Bo answered.

"Well, what is it?"

"What, what? I wanted some advice, that's all."

"About what?"

"You know," Bo said, blushing.

"Not yet I don't," Justin said, exasperated.

"About girls," Bo said, rolling his eyes.

"Girls?" Justin asked.

"Well," Bo said uncomfortably. "About one girl. Roan, actually."

Justin nodded and smiled, relaxing a little. "I see." He sat back in his chair and sighed.

"I just need some advice," Bo prompted. "You know, about women, and how you talk to them, and hang out with them."

"It's *women* now, is it?" Justin asked. "How to hang out with them? Hmmm. Well, I'd like to help, but I don't know if I'm the right person to ask," he said honestly, thinking of his sleepless night. His own perspective on relationships hadn't been exactly foolproof lately.

"What do you mean, you're not the right person to ask?" Bo wailed. "Justin, man, you're the coolest guy I know. You're practically the James Dean of Ocean City. You had the whole death scene—with a memorial on the beach and everything! Then a few days later you just show up in town again with no problem. It was very Bond," Bo said admiringly.

"I sense a theme. Maybe I should change my name to James," Justin said. Hero? He smiled wryly. Not in everyone's eyes.

"You had lots of girlfriends, didn't you?"

"Yeah, yeah," Justin admitted. "But that was a long time ago. I'm kind of out of the loop on that score."

"But you're dating Marta now," Bo pointed out.

"Well, yeah, I guess you could say that."

"Roan and I, we go for walks and all that," Bo explained. "But I want to know about talking. How to talk together."

"Well," Justin said, searching his mind. "I don't know quite what to tell you. To be honest, I never really went after women—"

"You mean they just flocked to you, right?" Bo said.

"I wouldn't say that, exactly," Justin said. "I was a lifeguard, don't forget. There are women who will fall in love with a lifeguard no matter what he looks like."

"So you can't tell me anything?" Bo asked.

"What's really the matter, Bo?" Justin replied. "Are you in some kind of a rush for any reason? Why are you so worried about it? Just take it slow."

"Man, it's dangerous being a guy," Bo answered. "What if I do something wrong? One minute things are fine, the next minute, they throw you out. You never know what's going to happen."

"Roan isn't going to throw you out." Justin laughed. "You're not renting, or hanging out. You live there."

"Yeah, so did Tosh, until yesterday," Bo muttered.

"What did you say?" Justin asked, his heart stopping for a moment.

"Yeah, he's outta there," Bo said. "Chelsea told me that Kate found him with some girl, in her own bedroom. Can you believe it?" Bo rolled his eyes. "I don't think I'm supposed to know, of course. Miss Perfect probably told them all not to say anything. But you know Chelsea. She's terrible at keeping secrets."

"Yeah, I know," Justin said, his mouth forming the words mechanically. His mind was somewhere else. For a moment, just a moment, he felt excited. Elated, actually. He felt like bursting out of his chair and running across the street and racing up to Kate's room, and—and—and what?

Hadn't he just told Bo that he was dating Marta? He liked Marta. She was beautiful. And fun. *And at the hospital—with Dominic,* a voice reminded him.

But for some reason, and Justin decided that he didn't want to think too closely about it, he suddenly felt his spirits pick up.

"Okay," Justin said, leaning forward. "About Roan—"

"Now we're getting down to business." Bo smiled.

"You like her?"

"Yeah," Bo said almost reverently. "I really like her a lot. It's just that every time we're together, my stomach gets all crazy and empty feeling. Sometimes," Bo admitted softly, "I feel like I'm going to hurl."

He looked around the apartment, as if to make sure no one was hiding behind any of the furniture.

"And I start sweating, you know," he went on, wiping his palms off on his shorts. "I'm even doing it now, just thinking about her."

"I guess you like her," Justin said, smiling. "But she's had it pretty tough, hasn't she? And not just recently."

"Yeah," Bo admitted. "She's had a hard time. I mean, she's really different from me. She's done a lot of things. She's been so many other places. I've never even been out of Ocean City except for vacation. Sometimes I worry that she's going to think I'm a total dweeb."

"I don't think you should worry about that," Justin advised. "I think maybe you should try not to think too much about what's happened to her before. Just be yourself with her. I think she needs to trust you, and if you act like yourself, she will."

"That's it, huh?" Bo asked. "That's the best advice I can get from King Stud of the Beach?"

Justin laughed. "Sorry, buddy. That's it."

"Be myself?" Bo complained. "But it's being myself that I want help with. I don't know *how* to be myself."

"Well, you'd better find out fast," Justin said. "Because that's the person she'll fall in love with."

"Yeah," Bo said. "Well, I hope so."

He stood up and went to the door.

"Thanks for the *advice*," Bo said sarcastically as he stepped outside. "I could have stayed home and watched *Oprah* for that."

"It's time for us to talk about where you're going to stay," Grace said, standing in the doorway of Roan's room. Her eyes moved over the small piles of Roan's belongings neatly folded on the bureau and waiting to be packed. There was also an extra bag by the door, full of the things Roan had swiped from Kate, Chelsea, and Marta.

"I guess so," Roan said softly, sitting on the edge of her bed.

"I'm glad to see that you took me seriously when I said it was time for you to go," Grace began, pointing to Roan's piles.

"Yeah," Roan answered.

"You know, I was really pissed off when I said that."

Roan looked up at her curiously.

"I've changed my mind for the time being," Grace went on. "And it may be because I'm feeling guilty right now, I don't know. But I'm not going to worry about it if you won't."

Roan shook her head.

"That means you can stay here," Grace continued. "If you want to. At least for now."

"Really?" Roan's voice was quiet, but Grace could hear the disbelief in it.

"Yes, really," she answered, smiling for a moment. "But this time," she said, "let's get the ground rules straight from the beginning. Number one: no drugs. It's illegal. And I have a brother and good friends who don't need that kind of trouble. Agreed?"

"Agreed."

"Number two," Grace went on, "no booze. And no booze means none. No liquor, no beer, no wine. This," Grace said, her eyes softening, "I know about. We don't need to discuss the draw. But just because I've been there, believe me, it doesn't mean I'm going to be sympathetic if you can't stay away. If you need help, you'd better go and get it. If it's a matter of self-control, then exercise it. Agreed?"

"Yeah," Roan answered earnestly. "Agreed."

"Good," Grace sighed. "Now my speech is over. I hope I wasn't too parental."

"No, no," Roan said quickly. "You were fine." She blushed. "I mean, you're right."

"I know that." Grace laughed. "What matters is that you know it too. By the way, am I still employing you?"

"I hope so." Roan nodded.

"You'll start again tomorrow?"

"Sure."

"Okay," Grace said, turning to leave. "The welcome wagon is moving on. You can put your clothes back."

"Grace?" Roan asked hesitantly as the door to her room started to shut.

"Yeah?" Grace poked her head back.

"I don't know how to do it all," Roan said uncertainly.

"Do what?" Grace asked, stepping back into the room.

"I don't know how to be normal. How to act without—without that stuff. Act like a girl should."

"You mean with boys?" Grace asked carefully.

Roan nodded uncomfortably. "I want to be good. Better than I've been for a long time."

Grace sighed. "Honestly? I don't think I'm the person to ask," she said wryly. "I'm just now figuring that out myself. If you need advice, maybe you should talk to Kate or Chelsea. They're both much closer to normal in that department."

Grace left Roan and went up to her room. She

stood by her bed, staring out at the sea. It was a bright, sunny afternoon. There were a few people tossing a Frisbee by the water. A man jogging with his dog. It was a good day. Ocean City was a good place.

At least it could be.

NINE

Justin watched the sailboats skim over the water in the bay. Marta had come with him to one of the docks close to the hospital.

"I'm so jealous," he sighed. "I'm beginning to feel out of place up here."

"You mean on land?" Marta laughed. "You look so sad, like a beached whale, or a turtle someone turned upside down."

Marta had finally let Justin drag her away from her bedside vigil for a stroll by the water. She'd brought some bread for the seagulls and was busily making little pellets and tossing them into the bay.

"I was out there for a long time," Justin said, shading his eyes against the sun. "It's a different way of life. I guess I really got used to it."

"Yeah," Marta sighed, pushing her wheelchair

along the sidewalk. "I think I know what you mean."

Justin caught up to her chair and smiled. He dropped his hand onto her shoulder.

"Have you ever been on a boat?" he asked.

"Once or twice when I was younger," Marta replied, remembering the feeling of freedom she'd had. "I've wanted to go," she admitted, "but most boats aren't equipped for the handicapped."

"You wouldn't need to take your chair," Justin pointed out. "As long as you had a life preserver. Besides, you're a good swimmer."

"That's true." Marta smiled. "Maybe I just haven't found someone with a boat who was comfortable enough to bring me along."

Justin sighed and looked back at the water. He watched a barefoot water-skier do a somersault.

"If I had my boat, I'd take you out," Justin said.

"I don't know if I'd trust you to come back," Marta said, tossing a bread ball into the air.

"Is it that obvious?" Justin asked. "I really miss it."

"You must be anxious to get Kate back, then," Marta said as she threw another bread ball and watched three seagulls dive for it.

"What?"

"I meant your boat," Marta lied. "Are you going to get it back?"

110

"Oh, right," Justin said. "I thought you meant . . . well, you know."

"What if I did?" Marta asked.

"I'm not," Justin answered sharply. "But I do miss my boat. I'm actually thinking about trying to rescue her," he admitted. "She's down in the Bahamas, somewhere. I'm going to try and call the consulate tomorrow when they open. Poor thing is probably dry-docked in some marina with a bunch of drug-running boats. I just hope they haven't scrapped her."

"Why would they do that?" Marta asked.

"Well, Grace isn't really clear on what went on down there," Justin explained. "But she seemed to think they'd said something about her claiming it, or releasing it, within a couple of months. She's not sure. That time may be up by now, and they may have auctioned it off or ripped it up for parts."

"I hope not." Marta smiled. "I remember you put a lot of work into her."

"I sure did." Justin sighed. "But anyway," he went on. "That may not be for a while yet, if there's even anything to go and rescue. So I guess for now I'll have to be content watching all the other lucky people out there." He swept his hand across the bay, and they both turned to watch the boats for a moment.

"Do you feel like eating?" Justin asked.

111

"Watching these seagulls is making me hungry."

"Oh yeah?" Marta asked. "Why didn't you tell me? There's enough to go around." She rolled up a bread ball and shot it at Justin's mouth. He tried to catch it, but it hit him in the nose instead.

"Real food?" he asked hopefully. "It'll be better than what you could get in the hospital cafeteria, anyway."

"Okay," Marta agreed, taking his hand. They started toward some of the bay-side restaurants.

"How are things at the hospital anyway?" Justin asked. "How's Dominic?"

"He's fine," Marta answered quickly. "The doctors say he'll be okay, and that he'll be ready to leave tomorrow. Actually," she said carefully, without looking at Justin, "he's going to come to Grace's house when he gets out. She offered to give him a place to stay."

"Huh?" Justin stopped walking.

"It's okay," she said quickly, squeezing his hand. "It doesn't have anything to do with us."

"If you say so," he replied.

"I do," she said strongly.

He leaned down to give her a kiss, and she kissed him back deeply, trying to reassure him. Or was she trying to reassure herself?

"I'm here to pick up the key for Hagen

Associates," Chelsea said to the woman at the front desk of the condominium unit.

"You're a bit early, aren't you?" The woman smiled. "They haven't had time to put fresh sheets on the bed," she added, giving Chelsea a card to sign in on.

"That's all right." Chelsea laughed. "Believe it or not, this is business. I'm not going to be using the bed."

"If you say so." The woman smiled again pleasantly. "It's a great little apartment. And the man who reserved it was pretty great looking himself," she said slyly, giving Chelsea a wink.

"Paul? He is," Chelsea agreed. "But I won't be working with him."

"Oh, sorry," the woman said. "Well, have fun anyway."

"Thanks."

The condo was really nice. Very homey and well-decorated. Bright, flowery upholstery on the living-room furniture. A neat, well-organized stand-up kitchen. The bedroom was the biggest room, with a draftsman's table and secretary desk at one end and a big queen-sized bed at the other.

Chelsea laid out her art supplies on the table, figuring the copywriter would want the desk. There was a fluorescent lamp, so she'd have good drawing light.

Chelsea checked her watch. It was now after five o'clock. The copywriter was officially late. She flopped down onto the big bed.

She was a bundle of nervous energy; excited to begin the project and full of preliminary ideas. Where was the damn copywriter! Chelsea started bouncing up and down on the bed. She hoped she wasn't stuck with an unreliable partner. Paul was giving them this first week to see what they could come up with. Chelsea knew he didn't want to have to direct them too much, just oversee and approve of their plans. So if this copywriter turned out to be a slacker, Chelsea was going to look bad as well.

Relax, she said to herself as she bounced higher and higher. *He's only ten minutes late. Everything is going to work out fine.*

"Whee!" she squealed as she bounced around the bed, her back to the door.

"Where do you think you are," a familiar voice said behind her, "the bloody circus?"

Immediately Chelsea stiffened and stopped bouncing. *It couldn't possibly be. No. No way. Oh, no!*

She turned slowly and found herself face-to-face with Connor.

"Connor—"

"Chelsea—"

"It's you," she said accusingly.

"You?" he squeaked. "What are you doing here?"

"Oh, no!" they said together.

"We can't—"

"I can't work—"

"—work together," Connor spluttered.

"—with *you*," Chelsea moaned.

"No way," they cried in unison.

They stood looking at each other warily. Chelsea couldn't believe it! How had Connor ended up here. On *her* job!

"You have to leave," she said angrily.

"What do you mean, *I* have to leave!" Connor demanded. "I think *you* need to go."

"This is *my* job," Chelsea snapped.

"It's *my* job," Connor countered.

"It was mine first," Chelsea argued.

"It was not!"

"Was too!"

"Not!"

"Too!" Chelsea shrieked. "When did *you* meet Paul?" she challenged.

"Wednesday!" Connor said. "He read some of my stuff and tracked me down at home. He said I was great."

"Hah! I met him Tuesday!" Chelsea crowed triumphantly. "He took me out to dinner and offered me a job."

"This job?" Connor probed.

Chelsea paused. "No," she admitted, "another job, actually."

"When did he offer you this one?"

"Saturday," she admitted.

"Hah! Saturday? It's mine!" Connor yelled.

"Oh yeah? This is my *second* job with him. I've got seniority. It's mine!"

"He took you out to dinner?" Connor asked suddenly.

Chelsea ignored him. "I'm not giving it up."

"Neither am I," Connor answered.

They tried to stare each other down, but it didn't work for either of them. They both sighed.

"I guess this means we'll be working together," Connor said softly.

"I guess so," Chelsea agreed.

Connor went over to the desk. He put his bag down and took out a few pencils and a notebook.

Chelsea went to the table and started fiddling with her supplies.

"What were you doing when I came in, anyway?" Connor finally asked, nodding at the bed. "Breaking it in for your unknown partner?"

"That's crude," Chelsea snapped, but she couldn't stop herself from blushing in embarrassment. "You're the one who was late."

"Well, I'm here now," Connor sighed. "And I guess we'd better start working."

"Yeah," Chelsea agreed, wondering how she was ever going to concentrate.

The answer was, she couldn't.

"How am I supposed to draw anything when I don't know what to draw?" she muttered an hour later. "I've gone through a ton of paper already, and I still don't know what I'm doing. I can't develop the art without knowing the words!"

She looked over to find Connor crumpling another piece of paper and tossing it onto the pile he was collecting in the corner.

"So it's my fault you can't draw anything?" Connor asked, turning around in his chair.

"You're the copy man," Chelsea said. "What's the hook?"

"The thing that gets stuck in the fish's mouth," Connor replied.

"Not for real, you idiot!" she snapped. "I mean the advertising hook. The gimmick. You haven't thought of one?"

"Is that all my job? I thought we were supposed to do this together."

"But you're the witty man of letters," Chelsea replied. "You had enough smart things to say to me. Are you telling me that you don't have anything left?"

"The way it works is that we *both* think of the gimmick. Then *I* write the copy and *you* draw the pretty pictures."

"All right," Chelsea said, standing up and turning her back on the mess she'd made of her sketchbook. "Let's think of a gimmick, then."

Connor stood also, stretching his arms above his head. He walked to the small kitchen, and Chelsea heard the sound of the refrigerator door opening and closing. Then all of the cabinets, one by one.

"Don't tell me you're going to try to find it in there," Chelsea yelled. "It's *supposed* to come from your brilliantly witty brain."

Connor came back into the room.

"I'm hungry," he said distractedly. He sighed. "How about 'The Fish-Lover's Friend'?" he suggested.

"Not the fish-lovers who want to protect the contents of the ocean," Chelsea replied. "How about 'Hook, Line, and Snapper'?"

"Do you want them to be afraid of their dinner?" Connor quipped.

Suddenly they were standing in front of each other by the bed. Chelsea watched as Connor's eyes focused on her, and for a brief moment she saw the longing in them, and recognized it. Before she could stop herself, she knew the same feelings showed in her own eyes. Connor was standing so close to her.

She had a sudden desire to touch him again. To feel him hold her. And then, as though she'd asked for it, she felt his arms come around her waist. The moment he touched her, there was a thrill. The same electricity she'd felt that first time last summer, when he'd kissed her on the beach, and later when she'd crept into his room in the middle of the night, curious and full of longing.

She closed her eyes as Connor's face neared hers. It truly was one of her favorite images. His handsome, lovely, freckled Irish face coming toward her.

She forgot all about the work they were supposed to be doing. The fact that they weren't living together anymore. All of the fights they'd had.

All Chelsea could think of as she hit the bed was that she was happy. And she was in her husband's arms again.

TEN

"How to Know When He Likes You, And What to Do About It!" the article in *Seventeen* read. Roan took a breath and sat poised on her bed, pen in hand, ready to take the test:

1. When he sees you coming, he

a) invites you to dinner and a movie.
b) smiles and asks how you've been.
c) nods and goes back to the conversation he was having.
d) excuses himself to go to the bathroom.

Even Roan could see that a) and b) were the best answers. This test didn't look too promising, especially since she was pretty sure that Bo did like her. And she knew that she liked him.

Maybe she ought to skip right to the part that told "What to Do About It." Although what *not* to do was more the kind of advice she needed. She was starting to flip the pages when someone knocked on her door.

"Who is it?" she asked.

"It's me, Bo," came the muffled reply.

Roan quickly closed the magazine and shoved it under her mattress.

"Come in," she said nervously.

The door opened and Bo came into her room.

"What are you doing?" he asked casually.

"Reading," she replied.

Bo looked around, and Roan realized she didn't have a book in her hand.

"I *was* reading," she explained, blushing. "I'm taking a break now."

"Do you want to go for a walk or something?" Bo asked.

"Oh." Roan shook her head quickly. "I don't know. I'm not feeling too good about walking around right now."

"Because of yesterday?"

She shrugged, embarrassed somehow to tell him that she was afraid. Afraid of running into Billy or any of his friends. Or any of Rick's friends.

"It's okay," Bo said. "Don't worry. The police have that guy. Besides, I'll protect you. We could walk on the beach right outside." He pointed to the door leading from her room to the terrace. "We'll stay by the house, if you want."

"Okay," Roan agreed. She had been feeling a little stir-crazy. She got up and grabbed her sweatshirt and pulled it on. They went out onto the terrace and then onto the sand, which was still a little warm from the sun that had been heating it all day. Bo took her hand, and Roan smiled, feeling much safer somehow.

They didn't go very far. Maybe only thirty or forty feet away from the house. Roan glanced behind her, and the warm glow from the windows reassured her.

"Do you want to sit?" Bo asked, dropping onto the sand.

Roan sat down beside him.

"You know," she said finally, "I've never really had a boyfriend. I know you think I probably have, but it's not true."

"It's okay," Bo replied. "I've never had a girlfriend, either."

"I mean, I know I told you that I've been with people—"

"I don't care," he interrupted.

"But I do," she said quickly. "I've never had a *real* boyfriend. You know, the kind who asks you out on dates and takes you places, like dinner. Or the movies. I've always wanted one like that," she admitted softly. "But I've never had one."

Bo reached out and took her hand in his.

"Maybe—" he began, and then stopped.

"Maybe what?" Roan asked, her voice hopeful.

"Maybe. Maybe I could do that," he struggled. "Take you out places or something. To the movies. If you wanted." He paused. "I wouldn't *have* to be your boyfriend," he said, taking his hand from hers when she didn't respond. "I mean, I could just be your friend."

Roan reached out and took his hand back in hers.

"You already are my friend, aren't you?" she asked, looking at him in the fading light.

He nodded.

"It's okay," she said, squeezing his hand. "I'd like you to be more. I just feel bad about . . . about how I was with you before."

She sighed, and thought of the few times they'd hung out together, when she'd been drunk or stoned.

"I don't want to be that way," she said softly. "It doesn't mean I don't still like you, though. I do."

"I like you, too," he replied, watching the water. "A lot."

"I'm glad." Roan slipped her shoes off and buried her feet in the sand.

"I'm not very experienced at that, though," Bo admitted. "I mean, asking a girl on a date."

"Maybe we can start over again," she suggested.

"You mean, like we just met?" Bo asked.

"Sure," Roan replied.

They heard the sound of laughter and looked down the beach. They saw a couple down by the water. The man was carrying the woman into the ocean. He dropped her into water up to her knees and she shrieked and ran away from him. He took off after her on the sand. Roan smiled.

"But I wouldn't be holding your hand if we just met," Bo pointed out.

"Okay. So we've known each other long enough to hold hands."

"And we're starting to date?" Bo asked.

"And we're just starting," Roan agreed. The sound of the ocean was soothing, and her feet were warm in the sand.

"Are we on a date now?" Bo asked.

"Do you want to be?" Roan asked.

"Yes," Bo said quickly. "But this isn't an official going-to-dinner-or-a-movie kind of date. Isn't that the kind you want?"

"Sure," Roan agreed. "So this isn't a date, then."

"So what is this?" Bo asked, his palms starting to sweat.

"This is a conversation, I guess," Roan said.

"A conversation about a date."

"Maybe," Roan answered. "I guess you have to ask me on a date first."

"Okay," Bo answered. "But give me a little time to think of one. All right?"

"All right." Roan smiled. A calm ocean breeze blew her hair back, and she squeezed Bo's hand gently. He squeezed back.

"Okay," Bo said, breathing easily. "Then I'll ask you on a date tomorrow."

"You don't have to tell me now if you're not asking me now," Roan said.

"But I don't want you to make plans." Bo laughed.

"I won't make any plans, then," Roan promised.

"Good. Then I'll see you tomorrow," Bo said.

"Yeah," Roan agreed. "I'll see you tomorrow."

They sat quietly listening to the ocean. Roan looked up and saw the stars starting to glimmer in the night sky.

"I hope tomorrow is as good as right now," Bo said, holding her hand tighter.

"I hope so too."

"Hmm," Chelsea sighed, burrowing into Connor's arms. "How about 'Feeding Frenzy'?"

"You know, the sharks eat each other when they do that, love," he murmured back. "Can you imagine a restaurant full of people going after one another with their forks and knives?"

"Yes," Chelsea said, squeezing closer to Connor. She could imagine anything now.

"Careful," he warned. "You're going to nudge me all the way off the bed."

Chelsea smiled. "Who would have thought?"

"I'm glad it was you," Connor agreed.

"Why, were you planning on using this bed no matter what?"

"No," he answered. "It just would have been a shame to let all the facilities in our pleasant working environment go unused."

"Well, the facilities aren't helping us much with the work."

"No," Connor admitted. "They're doing something much better."

Chelsea smiled. "How about 'Catch the Fever'? You know, *catch,* like a catch of fish."

"Or 'Catch a Fever for the Flavor of Fish,'" Connor suggested.

"Is that terrible?" Chelsea asked.

"I don't know," Connor said.

"We could do a follow-up ad too," Chelsea said, becoming intrigued by the idea. "Or you could just make it part of the copy. Like, 'Caught a fever for the taste of fish? Only we've got the cure: The Fishery.'" Chelsea laughed.

"'The Fishery: Where You'll Get a Bite,'" Connor said excitedly.

"'The Fishery: What a Catch!'" Chelsea challenged.

"'Where You and Your Team Can Win the

Game Against the "What's New?" Dinner Blues,'"
Connor responded.

"'Striped Bass,'" Chelsea countered.

Connor was about to go on, but he stopped.
"'Striped Bass'? I don't get it."

Chelsea held her arms out, pretending to play
a bass guitar. "Get it?" she said, laughing.

Connor's eyes widened. "Ahhh," he said. "I
get it."

"That's one where the *art* would make the
gimmick."

"I like that," he answered.

"What else could we do?" she asked.

"'Rock Lobster'?" Connor said.

Chelsea giggled, and threw her pillow at him.
Then she lunged and wrestled Connor to the
edge of the bed. She cried triumphantly just as
he was about to fall off. But suddenly, before she
knew it, he'd twisted away from her and she
found herself buried under his chest. *Not a terrible place to be,* Chelsea thought happily.

"You aren't sorry, are you?" Connor asked the
top of her head after he'd maneuvered her into
his arms.

Chelsea could hear his heart start to beat a little faster. Well, what had happened had taken
them both by surprise. They hadn't planned on
it, certainly. They hadn't planned on ending up
working together, of all things! But Chelsea

wasn't about to complain. And their foray into the bed had given them a burst of inspiration.

Perhaps they'd needed fate to step in for them. They were both too stubborn to admit that they had made a mistake in separating.

"I'm not sorry," she said. "Not even a tiny little bit."

"Good," he sighed. "That makes me very happy. I'm glad we're making up now. It's turned out to be great timing, actually."

"What do you mean?" Chelsea asked. "Were you getting ready to come apologize because you couldn't stand living without me anymore?"

"Apologize? Me?" Connor shook his head. "No, that's not why."

Chelsea stiffened at his response. "Why, then?" she asked.

"Because my parents are coming in a few days," he said casually.

"What!" Chelsea sat up, pulling the covers around herself. "What did you say about your parents?"

"That's right," he said, mistaking her surprise for nervousness. "My own mum and da. Direct from the homeland. I got a letter from them on Tuesday," he went on explaining, oblivious to Chelsea's growing anger. "It said they were coming in a week. So they'll be here Wednesday afternoon."

"Wednesday afternoon," Chelsea echoed, starting to shake.

"Yup," Connor said. "And am I ever glad you're going to be with me now. It was going to be awkward enough when they find out that you're black. At least now they won't find out you aren't living with me."

"You jerk!" Chelsea shrieked, smacking him hard in the head with a pillow and startling him enough to fall out of bed.

"What the—?" Connor yelled from the floor.

Chelsea slid from the bed and stepped quickly into her shorts. She yanked her shirt over her head.

Connor stood up with the sheets wrapped around him, an angry look on his face.

"What was *that* for?" he demanded.

Chelsea whirled to face him, wishing she could burn a hole through him with her gaze. He flinched when he saw her face.

"I can't believe you, you sneaky Irish snake!" she hissed.

"What did I do? What did I do that you didn't do? You were all over me! What was I supposed to do?" Connor cried.

"*I* was all over *you*?" Chelsea shrieked. "You are so typical! I can't believe you'd be so low. Making up with me because your folks are coming. 'Good timing, actually,'" Chelsea mocked.

"Good timing, my foot! And you never told them that I'm black! It's been a *year,* Connor. We've been *married* for a *year,* and you haven't told your parents that I'm black! Who the hell do they think you've married? Do they even know I'm not Irish?" she demanded.

"Well," Connor hedged, "I didn't go out of my way to say you weren't—"

"They think I'm white *and* Irish. What did you tell them my name was, Chelsea O'Lennox?"

"No," Connor said, looking hurt.

"Did you even *tell* them my *name*?"

"They know your name is Chelsea," Connor said defensively.

"Chelsea," Chelsea said. "That's it. Just, 'Mum and Da, I'm marrying Chelsea.' And they said, 'Okay, son, we're sure she's a fine white Irish girl.'"

"Look, it won't matter when they meet you," Connor whined. "Why give them something to worry about for no reason?"

"I'm their daughter-in-law!" Chelsea screamed. "That's no reason? And why would they worry, anyway? Are they racist or something?"

Connor winced. "Chelsea, they're not racist. You don't understand. There are practically no black people in all of Ireland. My parents have probably never even met a black person. It doesn't mean they're racist. They come from a very small village. They're conservative because

130

they haven't experienced much. Why give them time to worry and concoct fantasies when they can just *meet* you in person and see that you're fine."

"That I'm fine," Chelsea echoed. "You mean human? Two arms, two legs, one head, fine?"

"No!" Connor exploded. "Not fine. Wonderful. When they meet you, they'll see that you're wonderful!"

"Well, you'll have to tell them yourself," Chelsea barked back at him. "Because they won't be meeting me! I'm onto your games, Riordan. I know what all of this," she swept the room with her arm, "was about. You were in a jam, so once again you find a way to manipulate your way out of it. Well, forget it. I won't be used like that. You've lied to your parents. You'll have to deal with it yourself now. We are *not*, I repeat *not*, back together!"

"So I guess you're going to throw this job away now too," Connor challenged. "Running away without finishing again?"

"I am not giving up this job," Chelsea said coldly.

"Right," Connor said stormily.

"This relationship will be strictly professional. I don't care what goes on in your *private* life," Chelsea sneered. "I'm not interested in hearing any more lies."

"Well, I think we've done more than enough 'work' tonight," Connor snapped. "I for one couldn't take any more."

"Fine," Chelsea replied, grabbing her bag and heading for the door. "I'll see you tomorrow night at six P.M. Don't be late," she demanded. "And plan to keep your clothes on next time," she said, slamming the door behind her.

ELEVEN

"So Grace tells me that you're looking for a way to get down to the Bahamas," David said, wiping his hands on a rag hanging from his waist. He'd just finished giving a morning flying lesson, and he was going over the engine of his Cessna, checking all the lines and levels.

On Grace's suggestion, Justin had run out to the little airport to ask David if he had any leads on flights going down to the islands.

"Yeah," Justin said. "I called there this morning, and it seems that my little baby is still in one piece, although she was about to be scheduled for disassembly."

"That sounds ominous," David said.

"Sure does." Justin cringed, remembering how relieved he'd felt when he found out his boat was still safe. "So obviously I'd like to get down there as soon as possible. Grace mentioned you might know of some pilots heading in that general direction."

"Don't go for the general direction." David laughed. "You definitely want someone to take you exactly where you need to go. It's pretty hard to hitchhike in the sky. And pilots aren't allowed to just dip out of their way as a favor."

"I'm just trying not to be pushy," Justin admitted with a smile. "If you know of someone going to the Bahamas, I'd be grateful for the tip."

"As it happens," David said, smiling, "I do know someone headed in that *exact* direction. Grace and I are flying with him in two days. He's dropping us off in Georgia, and then he's going on to the islands. He's got a little sweetheart he met down there."

"Are you kidding?" Justin asked.

"What? About the sweetheart?" David asked. "No way. That's very serious."

"No," Justin said. "I meant about the Bahamas. I can't believe how lucky that is. Lucky for me, anyway."

David wiped his hands on the rag and nodded. "I guess it is lucky. If it's not short notice."

"Not at all," Justin replied. "I'll take what I can get. I don't imagine that the airway between O.C. and the Bahamas is all that well traveled."

"You'd be surprised," David said, laughing.

"My friend alone travels it often enough to book himself as a regular airline."

Justin took the wrench David handed him and dropped it into the toolbox at his feet.

"What are you going to Georgia for, anyway? You don't have relatives there, do you?" Justin asked skeptically.

"No way," David snorted. "My family is from Brooklyn. None of them would ever leave New York. This is just a little business venture for Grace. She's keeping it under wraps, though," David warned, "so don't try getting any inside information from me. I'm only going along for the ride."

"It would be great if I could come along, too," Justin said. "How much do you think your friend would need?"

"You mean how much money?" David asked.

"Sure," Justin said.

"It wouldn't cost you a thing. Like I said, he's a friend of mine. Besides, he'd probably be willing to pay for the company. It's a long flight. You can keep him awake. Or he can keep you awake. He's quite a storyteller."

"In two days?" Justin asked again.

"Wednesday, noon. Try and get here around eleven, just to be on the safe side. We might get an earlier flight slot."

"Thanks, David," Justin said. "I appreciate it more than you know."

"Oh, I know all right," David said, lovingly patting the nose of his little plane. "I know what she means to you. Different medium," he admitted with a smile, "but the same freedom."

Justin smiled. "See you in two days," he said, turning and beginning the long run home. "Oh, wait a minute," he stopped himself and called back.

David looked out from behind the engine of the plane.

"What about Mooch?" Justin yelled.

"Your dog?" David asked.

"Yeah. Can he come along too?"

"If you get a cage for him, it should be fine. As long as he can be strapped down. Is he used to traveling?" David asked, wrinkling his nose. "Because if he's not, you might want to bring some extra paper towels and garbage bags."

Justin laughed. "Don't worry about Mooch. He spent nine months on a boat. He won't get sick."

Justin turned away and ran across the tarmac to the airport exit. Well, he didn't have too much to organize before he went. Some supplies, and a pack of tools and replacement parts. No job to worry about. No housing commitment. Connor would probably welcome his couch back, and a dog-free environment.

And he wasn't too worried about saying

good-bye to Marta. She knew how much he wanted to be sailing again. And he knew by now that he certainly wasn't going to break her heart. Whatever she said, Justin was convinced that she still had some strong feelings for Dominic. She wouldn't miss him much.

Neither would Kate, for that matter. And that thought made him restless. It made him want to leave Ocean City forever. It was just too hard to be near her. Especially when she wasn't with someone else. When there was no *good* reason she wasn't with him. So it was time for him to leave. Get back to his boat, the *Kate* he could have, and keep sailing. It was what he'd always wanted to do anyway.

If the seas of the world couldn't fill the emptiness in his heart, Justin thought sadly, nothing else ever would.

Monday afternoon Marta signed Dominic out of the hospital. Grace and Roan and Bo came with her to help get him home. The nurses put him in a wheelchair, and Bo pushed him outside to the parking lot.

The sun was bright, and Dominic squinted against the glare.

"Here," Roan said, holding her sunglasses out to him. "You can wear these back to the house if you want."

"Thanks," he said softly, waving her hand away. "I'll be fine."

Bo pushed Dominic's wheelchair to Marta's specially equipped van.

"I'm glad I finally know someone who gets to park in the handicapped zone," Bo huffed, breathing heavily. "Because this chair is heavy."

"Bo," Grace snapped.

"That's all right." Marta laughed, rolling herself out of the hot sun. "There aren't many benefits, but parking spaces are one of them."

The lift on the van door raised Dominic's chair up, and Bo pushed the wheelchair forward to lock in place on the passenger side. Marta maneuvered herself into the driver's seat. She looked over and saw Dominic staring at his wheelchair lined up next to hers, a look of horror on his face.

"Ironic, isn't it?" she asked tightly.

Dominic shook his head and looked away. "Like a nightmare," he whispered.

Grace poked her head through the window.

"We'll follow you home in case you need help there," she said. "Although our house is now pretty well equipped for wheelchairs, so I'm sure you won't have much trouble."

Marta knew everyone else thought it was rather amusing to have two wheelchair-bound housemates. Well, as amusing as a stabbing could be.

Marta, too, would have found it funny if it hadn't been Dominic in the other wheelchair.

"The house is well-equipped," Marta agreed, starting up the van. "But our new guest isn't as good a driver as I am."

Grace laughed and squeezed her arm.

"See you at home," she called out as Marta drove away.

By the time Grace, Roan, and Bo had returned, Marta had managed to direct Dominic out of the van, into the house, and down the elevator. None of it came without a certain amount of difficulty. But watching Dominic struggle made Marta feel better somehow, though she knew it shouldn't.

Now here he was in her house, having to get along like she did. Like she had every day of her life for the past six years. She was allowed some measure of satisfaction, wasn't she? After all, no one was completely above a little revenge if they could get it. It was almost like a cosmic joke, that Dominic would end up in a wheelchair with Marta as his nurse.

Roan's room was next to Marta's downstairs, and Roan had donated her bed for the new guest. Bo and Grace had moved it into Marta's room that morning.

"Now put yourself next to the bed," Marta instructed when she finally got Dominic into her room. She rolled over and helped him adjust the chair. Then she locked the wheels in place and went around to the other side. She locked her own wheels and stretched out her arms to him across the bed.

"Give me your hands," she said calmly.

Dominic reached out, and Marta grabbed him around the wrists.

"Fireman's hold," she said, indicating that he grab her wrists. "Ready? One, two, three!" She took a breath and yanked. With the strong muscles in her shoulders and back, Marta lifted him quickly and easily. Within seconds he was out of the chair and onto the bed.

"You're pretty strong," he panted, clinging to the sides of the bed weakly.

"I have reason to be," she replied.

"I knew that," he answered softly. "But this is the first time I've felt how strong you are myself."

That's not true, Marta thought before she could stop herself. *You felt me in your arms that night on the pier.* Immediately she shook her head and chased the thought away. She pulled the light blanket over him and helped prop up his pillow.

"Why don't you get some sleep," she instructed. "I'll bring you some food a little later."

Chelsea was out on the deck sketching bass

guitars and dancing fish in her notebook when Roan found her.

"What's all that for?" she asked.

"This job I'm doing," Chelsea replied, scowling. "For a seafood restaurant."

"Oh, I see. Am I interrupting?"

"Do you want to be?" Chelsea said lightly, taking the hint and happily putting away her work. Anything not to have to think about Connor and last night's total fiasco. "It's a beautiful, sunny day," Chelsea said, reaching for her sunglasses. "And I for one would rather talk than work on a sunny day."

"I actually wanted to ask your advice on something," Roan began, sitting down stiffly on the edge of one of the lounge chairs. "Grace thought you'd be able to help me."

"With what?" Chelsea asked curiously.

"With guys," Roan admitted.

"Grace thought *I* could help you?" Chelsea burst out laughing. "She must have been pulling your leg. Grace knew more about guys as a freshman in high school than I'll probably ever know in my entire life! Roan, I was a *virgin* when I got married."

"Grace told me that already," Roan said, looking away.

"Grace told you about my sex life?"

"Yeah," Roan replied, looking embarrassed.

141

"What do you think I can tell you about guys, then? How to go to church and stay away from them until you marry?" Chelsea asked.

Roan shook her head, blushing.

"I'm not talking about sex," Roan explained. "Although that's one reason I want to talk to you, and why Grace can't be much help."

"You're not talking about sex," Chelsea repeated.

"No. I want to know how to be with guys in a normal way. A better way. Everything you should do *before* sex. I want to have a normal relationship, and Grace said that you and Kate are much more normal when it comes to guys."

Chelsea laughed. She couldn't help it. She'd thought this conversation would help her *stop* thinking about Connor.

"Kate is definitely normal," Chelsea agreed. "But, Roan," she continued, "is it normal for a virgin to marry an illegal alien of a different race as an eighteen-year-old, only to separate from him one year later?"

"Did you love him when you married him?" Roan asked.

Chelsea sighed. She didn't dare answer that question, because she still loved him. That was the problem.

"What do you want to know?" Chelsea asked seriously.

"I want to go slowly," Roan answered. "And I want to know *how* to do that."

"I still don't think I can be very helpful," Chelsea said. "You really should try Kate. I'm not the specialist at thinking things through clearly, but I'll try to give you what advice I can. Are we talking about Bo, by the way?"

"Yeah," Roan admitted.

"Well, he seems nice enough," Chelsea said. "Listen, Roan, I believe in love. If an artist isn't a romantic, then who will be? But the best advice I can give you," she paused and took a breath, "is *whatever you do, don't trust them!*"

Roan flinched. "Really?"

"Come on, Roan. What just happened to you? You were led astray, by *men*. *Men* tried to take advantage of you. It was a *man* who tried to stab you, wasn't it? Are these coincidences? I don't think so. Even the nice ones, Roan," Chelsea went on, her eyes turning steely as she thought of Connor, "even the nice ones. The nice ones are the ones you have to watch the closest. Because they say sweet things to you. And they make you think they really care." Chelsea's eyes began to blaze. She was holding a pencil in her hands so tightly that her knuckles were turning white.

"And then, when you've *completely* forgiven them," the pencil in her hands snapped in two, and Chelsea paused and looked at Roan, whose jaw had dropped in shock, "you find out they had some ulterior motive all along. They're manipulators, that's what they are."

"Wow," Roan breathed.

"I'm sorry, Roan," Chelsea said, shaking her head. "But someone needs to tell you before you find out the hard way."

Marta brought Dominic hot soup for lunch. He was still too weak to sit up. Although he didn't want her to, Marta insisted on feeding him. She spooned the broth into his mouth carefully, as she would for any patient.

He finished the soup, and Marta was wheeling away when he called to her.

"Marta," he said tentatively.

"Yes," she replied, turning her chair around easily and wheeling back to his side.

"Do you think you could get Tosh to come down here for a minute?" he asked her casually.

Marta shook her head. "Tosh moved out."

"What about Bo, then?"

"I think he went shopping with Grace."

Dominic was turning red. "Is there a phone here?"

"Can I call someone for you?" Marta asked innocently.

"Could you please call Connor or Justin?"

"Dominic, you'd better tell *me* what you need." She was pretty sure what the problem was, but she wasn't going to make this easy.

"What I need?" Dominic rolled his eyes. His face was burning red. "I need to go to the bathroom, is what I need!" he exploded.

Marta nodded. "I thought so."

"You thought—?" Dominic looked at her, and fell quiet.

"I was wondering how long you'd be able to hold out," she admitted.

"I need *help*," Dominic said carefully.

"Try and sit up for a moment, and I'll help you into your chair," Marta instructed.

Dominic sighed, and struggled to his elbows. Marta grabbed him under his armpits and helped slide him from the bed into his wheelchair.

"Follow me," she said. "I'll show you how to get on and off the toilet."

Marta rolled over to the bathroom and opened the door. She turned to say something to Dominic, but he wasn't behind her. He hadn't moved from the side of the bed. His head was in his hands, and Marta could see his shoulders shaking a little. He was crying.

"Dominic," she said sternly. "Come over here."

He looked up at her and quickly wiped his eyes in embarrassment. Then he slowly pushed his chair over to her.

"Do you see the bars along the wall?" she asked him.

He nodded.

"Watch how I do this. If you're not used to it, it can be pretty tricky."

Marta rolled herself into the bathroom, placing her chair as close to the seat as she could. She used her right hand for leverage below her on the toilet seat, and with her left hand she grabbed the rail. She pulled and lifted herself out of her chair and turned herself around in midair before dropping softly onto the toilet seat.

"There!" she said, facing the doorway.

Dominic looked utterly mortified.

"Believe me," she said, chuckling. "It's that exciting when you can do it right. Maybe you'll need to end up on the floor a few times to appreciate it." Marta shifted back into her wheelchair and rolled out of the way to give Dominic room.

"You're not going to stay, are you?" he asked in a small, horrified voice.

"I've seen it before, Dominic," Marta said impatiently. "You might need some help."

Dominic wheeled his chair over to the toilet.

"Closer," Marta instructed, "and at an angle. You'll have better leverage if the rail is in front of you. It'll be easier on your arms."

Dominic grabbed the railing and put one hand on the toilet seat. He tried to lift and pull himself as Marta had done, but he couldn't do it as quickly or as cleanly, and his chair started sliding away beneath him.

"You didn't brake your wheels," Marta said, rolling over and bracing Dominic's chair with her own. He was hanging between his chair and the toilet seat, and he couldn't quite pull himself up. Marta saw his arms starting to shake and knew he was about to collapse. She reached out and grabbed him under the arms again, helping to lift him onto the toilet.

"It's not so easy, is it?" she asked.

"It's hard," he whispered. "Too hard."

"Now you know how I live," Marta said before she could help herself.

She could see at that moment that he understood. Understood why she had offered to take care of him. Understood why she wanted him nearby.

"I'm beginning to know," he said quietly.

TWELVE

"Well," Bo said. "It's Monday night. Do you know where your date is?"

He was standing in the doorway of Roan's room, wearing a clean pair of jeans and a freshly washed T-shirt.

"I was beginning to wonder," Roan replied. She was sitting carefully on the cot that Grace had put in her room, since she'd donated her bed to Dominic. "I was just thinking I'd have to go upstairs and poke around for you in the garage."

"Oh, don't call it that," Bo said.

"Don't call what what?" Roan asked.

"Don't call my room a garage," Bo said, feigning hurt. "A garage is where you store all your broken bicycles and old lawn mowers. Not where your date lives."

"But it is a garage," Roan said, laughing.

"Maybe," Bo admitted. "But it also happens to be skateboard heaven. And the coolest room in this house."

"Oh?" Roan said. "I disagree." She pointed to the door that led to the patio. "I have access to the beach."

"I know," Bo replied easily.

Roan remembered last night and smiled.

"Alright already," she finally said. "Where are we going? Or better yet," she looked at the clock, "are we going?"

"Going where?"

"I don't know," Roan cried. "That's what you're supposed to tell me."

"Oh, right." Bo laughed. "Our date. But I haven't asked you yet."

"No," Roan admitted, sighing. "Not *yet!*"

"Okay, okay," he said.

Bo bent over and bowed deeply to her. "Would you like to accompany me on a date this evening?" he asked in a serious voice.

"Where to?" Roan asked shyly, putting her hand to her hair, which had been carefully French-braided by Chelsea earlier.

"Very conventional," Bo replied. "A movie."

Roan checked her watch again. "I was wondering when you were going to come down here," she teased. "I've been ready for about an hour."

"That will teach you, then, won't it?" he said, looking around her room. "What did you do down here for an hour, anyway?" he asked.

"You don't want to know all my secrets, do you?" Roan asked.

Bo glanced at her, and she could see the appreciation in his eyes.

"Nah," he said. "Don't tell me. Whatever you did was worth it. You look great."

Roan smiled. She was definitely feeling good tonight. And it was Bo who made her feel that way. As though she was a normal girl, like any other sixteen-year-old. But then she remembered what Chelsea had told her that afternoon. Bo *was* nice, Roan knew, but she didn't want to be tricked into anything. And it made sense, as Chelsea had said, that the nicer they were, the harder it would be to see when they were using you.

"Bo," Roan said carefully. "I want to get something straight before we leave."

"Okay," Bo said. "You sound pretty serious. Should I sit down?"

"No, that's all right. I just think we should decide together what's going to happen tonight. I think that we need to be careful. So I'd like us to hold hands, if you want, but nothing else. All right?"

"Okay," he said, nodding. "No problem."

"Can I ask what's playing?" Now that Roan

had laid out the ground rules, she wanted to get past them as quickly as possible.

"*Lethal Weapon Number Something,*" Bo said. "I forget. But there are two other movies, if that's no good."

"No, that's fine," Roan agreed.

"You haven't seen it already?"

Roan shook her head. "I haven't seen *Lethal Weapon Number Anything.* Will that matter?"

"Nah," Bo said. "They're very self-contained movies. The best ones always are."

"Okay. Just one more thing to get straight before we go."

"What now?" Bo cried, eyes wide.

"Do you eat popcorn?" Roan asked, smiling.

"Is that a do-I as in do-I-always or is it a do-I as in would-I-if-you-wanted-some?"

"It's a do-you as in do-you-always."

"Nope."

"Good," Roan sighed. "Because I hate sitting in the movies with people who eat popcorn. The sound drives me crazy!"

"Well, I'm glad I passed *that* very important requirement. Can we go now?"

"Yes. Sorry. Am I ruining it?" Roan asked.

"I think we're still okay." Bo smiled. "Barely. Are you ready?"

"Are we walking?"

"It seems like a nice night for a walk."

"Okay, let me get my coat."

"Do I seem like myself to you?" Bo asked.

"Not really," Roan admitted. "Do I?"

"I wouldn't recognize you if I weren't looking at you," Bo said. "It must be the date."

"I'm giddy," Roan admitted. "And I'm not even on anything."

This is what love must be like, she thought. Then Bo reached for her hand.

"You did say holding hands was okay, right?" he checked.

Roan nodded, lacing her fingers with his.

Justin went across the street to Grace's house at six o'clock. He was hoping that he wouldn't run into Kate. When the front door opened as he approached, he held his breath and debated ducking into the bushes. But it was only Bo and Roan.

"Hey, Justin." Bo smiled at him happily.

"Hi." Roan nodded.

"Going out?"

"Movies," Bo said. "Thanks for the talk yesterday."

"Anytime." Justin waved.

From what he could see, Bo was doing pretty well. Justin definitely approved of Roan's new, more natural approach to makeup and hairstyles. *At least my advice works for some people,* he thought. Something told him as he went into the house that his dinner with Marta wasn't going to work out the way he hoped.

He went downstairs and found Marta in her room with Dominic. Justin watched them from the doorway. He would have bet money that the beautiful dark-haired woman in the wheelchair was in love with the handsome dark-haired guy on the bed. Even if the woman herself had told him differently.

"Marta?" he said softly.

She turned to the door, and Justin was sure that her face reddened when she saw him. But she smiled quickly and nodded for him to come in.

"Dominic." Justin smiled generously. "Good to see you out of the hospital."

"Thanks," Dominic said softly. "I don't mean to keep Marta," he said quickly. "She's insisting—"

"I'm sitting right here," Marta said irritably. "I hate when people talk about someone as though they aren't there. I'll bring you dinner when I come back," she said to Dominic, who closed his eyes and let his head fall against the pillows.

"Come with me to the den for a minute," she said, leading Justin out of her room.

"I know I said we'd have dinner," Marta began apologetically as soon as she had shut the door behind her. "But I can't leave him yet. No one else in the house really knows how to deal with him except me."

"That's all right." Justin smiled. "To be honest, I kind of expected this."

"You know there's got to be some food upstairs in the fridge, and if you want to stay awhile, maybe we can go for a walk later," Marta offered.

"Sounds good," Justin replied.

"Food first," Marta said cheerfully. "I know you can help yourself. You've got legs," she snickered, pinching him as a reminder.

Justin went upstairs to the kitchen and found Grace standing in front of the fridge.

"What's wrong, Racey?" Justin asked, laughing. "Nothing appealing?"

Grace turned and smiled.

"Nothing but you," she joked. "I'm just facing the common dilemma of what to eat on my nachos: medium salsa or spicy salsa."

"That's a tough one," Justin agreed. "You sure you don't want to go for something exotic, like bean dip?"

"Now that's an idea." Grace's eyes sparkled. "And if you want to make them, I'll let you have half."

"I'll cook for you anytime," Justin said gallantly as Grace moved away from the fridge.

"What have we got here?" he muttered, rifling through the multitude of plastic bags. "Cheddar cheese," he said, handing the bag to Grace.

"Bean dip. Salsa—medium and spicy. Olives. Aha!" he cried, pulling something from the fridge and standing up. "What's this? Sour cream?"

"Wait, wait," Grace cried as Justin went to take off the lid. "Check the date first—"

"Ohhh." Justin fell back against the counter, covering his face with his arm. "Too late," he moaned. "Here, you read it." He flung the top of the container at Grace. "What does it say?"

"Hmmm." Grace read the numbers. "It's not so bad," she said defensively.

"Grace?"

"April."

"Grace!" Justin cried. "That's practically three months old. I'm surprised Kate didn't throw it away six weeks ago. She usually tosses things right on their expiration dates."

"I guess she's been distracted." Grace smirked.

"Right," Justin said, turning back to the food. "Well, throw that—whatever it is—away and grate some cheddar."

Justin pulled out a pan and arranged a layer of chips on it while Grace stood next to him, shredding cheese. He was cutting tomatoes when Kate walked through the kitchen door.

"Hi, Kate," Grace said happily. Justin put down his knife and turned around carefully. Kate came in and tossed her bag onto the table.

"Justin was just wondering how you could have left the sour cream in our refrigerator for so long," Grace said casually.

"Justin?" Kate looked over at him. "What are you doing here?" She fell into a chair and pushed off her sneakers.

"Hi, Kate." Justin nodded, struggling to keep his voice steady. She looked incredible, with her blond hair wild from a long day on the beach, and a dark tan that made her hair seem even more golden.

"Oh, yeah," Grace added, looking at him. "I hadn't got around to asking you that yet."

"I was going to have dinner with Marta," Justin admitted quietly. "But she's sort of on call right now, and I doubt she'll get away."

"You mean the Salgado Hospice downstairs?" Grace chuckled. "She's very equipped down there. Maybe I should let her open a clinic."

"Speaking of which," Justin looked over at Kate, "how's your foot?"

"It's fine."

"So I hear you're going to be flying with us?" Grace said to Justin. "Can you cook and talk at the same time, by the way?" she added. "I'm starving."

"Flying?" Kate said quickly. "Where to?"

"The Bahamas," Justin said. Their eyes met for a brief moment, and then they both looked quickly away.

156

"He's going to get his boat. *Kate*," Grace added unnecessarily. "You remember. The other woman?"

"Grace," Justin warned.

"I remember," Kate said. "So you're getting your boat back? That's great."

Justin turned to look at her, but she wouldn't meet his gaze. "Yeah," he said. "I'm anxious to get back to the ocean."

"And I'm anxious to eat some dinner," Grace said. "Throw on that cheese and let's get these babies going."

They heard someone stomping down the stairs, and all three looked up to find Chelsea walking into the kitchen with a scowl on her face.

"Chels?" Kate asked. "Are you okay?"

"Hmph," Chelsea muttered.

"How's the condo?" Grace asked.

"Hmph." Chelsea went to the cupboard above the stove, pulled out a box of Pop-Tarts, and put two foil-wrapped packages in her bag.

"Is that your dinner?" Justin asked. "You can have some of our nachos."

"If they ever get finished," Grace said.

"Is something going wrong with your job for Paul Hagen?" Kate asked.

"Paul Hagen?" Justin said, the name sounding very familiar.

Chelsea grunted and picked up her bag.

"How's the copywriter?" Kate pressed. "I'm sorry, Chelsea, is he no good?"

"Copywriter?" Justin echoed dumbly.

"He's a liar and a jerk," Chelsea muttered as she went out the door, "but what else is new?"

The front door slammed behind her. Kate and Grace looked at each other, stupefied.

"It's Connor," Justin finally explained. "He's working for Paul Hagen too."

"You're kidding." Grace snorted. "That's perfect."

"That's terrible," Kate said. "After all that happened, to find themselves suddenly together—" Kate's eyes met Justin's, and the words died in her mouth.

"Pretty smooth, Kate," Grace said.

"You're right, though," Justin said stiffly. "It is uncomfortable. I'm sorry. This is your house," he said to Kate. "I'll go."

"No, no," Kate said quickly. "I didn't mean it. I mean, I didn't mean you. I'm going upstairs anyway. Please, just forget it."

"Fine," Justin said, picking up the bean dip and salsa. But he knew that that had been his problem all along. He couldn't forget it. He just couldn't forget her.

"I told Grace you were really from Georgia, and she couldn't believe it." Bo laughed. The movie was over, and he and Roan were walking home along the boardwalk. "She called you a Southern belle."

"My mother isn't like those people," Roan said sadly. "She doesn't think enough of herself."

"It doesn't matter to me," Bo told her. "I'm just glad you're here, and not down in Georgia wearing hoop skirts, carrying a fan, and drinking iced tea or something."

"That must have been a movie you saw. If I was down in Georgia I'd be wearing rags, carrying a knife, and drinking whiskey or something." She tried to laugh, but it caught in her throat and ended up sounding more like a whimper. Bo tightened his grip on her hand.

They paused on the edge of the boardwalk. The house was only a few hundred feet away. But from where they stood they had a clear view of the ocean and the canopy of stars above them.

Bo turned to face her and took Roan's other hand in his, so that he was holding both of them.

"If this is all I can do," he said by way of explanation. He looked at her in the moonlight, and his heart started pounding in his chest. She was more beautiful than usual, and her dark-brown eyes seemed even larger.

"I wish I could kiss you," he finally whispered.

"I wish I could kiss you, too," Roan admitted, leaning her forehead against his.

They were close enough to feel each other's breath on their faces.

"I've just been so messed up," Roan said. "I really want to do this right." She looked up at him. "It's important to me" was all she could say.

"We'll do it right," Bo said, squeezing her hands in his. "Have I told you your hands are my favorite thing about you?"

"So you're going to rescue her, huh?" Marta asked when she and Justin were finally alone together.

They had decided to take a walk near the house. It was late, and somehow Marta sensed that it wouldn't be a very long conversation. There was a warm breeze, and the air was full of the soft sound of the leaves rustling in the trees.

"Yep," Justin replied. "I'll be leaving in two days."

"Two days?" Marta asked. The realization that she wasn't upset didn't surprise her.

"David has a friend who's flying down there, so I can catch a ride for free. And she's still there, so I'd better do something fast before she gets taken away," Justin explained.

Marta nodded. "I agree, Justin. Especially if you're leaving. You'd better do something fast, or you will lose her. For good."

"I know," Justin said defensively. "But I've

only been home a week. I'm getting down there as fast as I can."

"Justin," she tried again. "We're not talking about the boat anymore, and you know it."

"What?" he asked, but Marta shot him a don't-give-me-that-routine look. "Kate," he said simply.

"Yes, Kate. Kate the woman. The one who's in the house behind us. You remember her, don't you? The one you wanted to sail away with? Are you sure you don't miss her?"

"No, I guess I'm not sure." Justin sighed. "I'm sorry."

"You don't have to apologize to me," Marta said. She liked Justin a lot, but didn't this mean it was over between them? It should be. They couldn't stay with each other. He was still in love with Kate.

And herself? She had no ulterior motives. She just didn't want to be someone's backup girl-friend. That was all.

"You *are* in love with her, right?" Marta pressed.

"I am," Justin admitted. "I guess I still am. Not that I should be, because we don't have any future together. Too bad my heart doesn't understand that." He took Marta's hand.

"I hope you're not mad at me," he said. "I really think you're wonderful."

"I think you're wonderful too," Marta said.

"I guess we both had the same problem," Justin mused. "Maybe that's why we were drawn together."

"What problem?"

"Loving people we think we don't want to love anymore."

"What do you mean?" Marta asked defensively.

"You know who I mean, Miss Nightingale. Your new patient?"

"No way," Marta said quickly. "I know what you're thinking, but it's not the same for me and Dominic."

"I can see how it might seem like a betrayal to yourself to love him," Justin pressed. "But if he makes you happy now—"

"No!" Marta interrupted. "No," she said more softly, shaking her head. "You're wrong, Justin. I'm sorry, but it just isn't that easy. It's *your* heart that won't listen to reason," Marta reminded him, "not mine."

"If you say so," Justin said.

"I do," Marta said determinedly.

"You've been a good friend, Marta," Justin said, reaching out and stroking her cheek.

Marta smiled, and Justin leaned down and kissed her gently on the lips. There was as usual the small spark. They'd always found each other attractive. But somehow, at the important moments, they'd both thought of being somewhere else.

"You'll make a great doctor," Justin said as he pulled away. "Don't be so stingy with that kind of medicine. I can think of a patient or two who could really use it."

"I'll figure out the prescriptions, Dr. Garrett, thank you very much," Marta said only half-jokingly.

"Okay," Justin said. "I get the message. It's not my place anymore."

"I'll always take advice from a friend," Marta countered, squeezing his hand.

"I'm glad I am one," Justin smiled.

"You should be," Marta replied.

"You are going to try and get the last word in, aren't you?"

"Of course. My last words are the best."

"You've never heard mine," Justin said.

"And I never will."

"You're sneaky."

"Determined."

"That's what I admire about you."

"Then you're smarter than you look."

"Thank you. I'll remember that."

"Just remember me."

"Good night," Justin said.

"Good-bye," Marta said, wheeling away.

"And good luck," they both called back at the same time, laughing as they each headed away into the darkness.

THIRTEEN

"You look like you're feeling much better," Marta remarked as she brought Dominic breakfast the next morning.

"I am, thanks," he agreed, pushing himself into a sitting position. "Now it feels as though I'm being given breakfast in bed, instead of needing breakfast in bed."

Marta smiled tightly. Breakfast in bed was something you did for your boyfriend. She suddenly felt embarrassed by the attention she'd paid to making up the tray for him. It was true, she thought. It was as though she was giving it to him by choice.

"Well, I'm glad to see that you can do it yourself." She dropped the tray into his lap.

"Marta?" Dominic asked, his face full of concern. "Is something wrong?"

"Obviously not," she replied. "You're getting well, that's all. Pretty soon you'll be well enough to go."

She turned away then, but not before seeing his dark eyes flash with pain. It was the first time since the stabbing that she had reminded him of his promise to leave Ocean City. Perhaps he'd thought things had changed. Well, he was mistaken then. A few days in a wheelchair wasn't going to change the past, Marta thought.

When she came back later to collect the tray, Dominic was sitting up in bed, waiting for her.

"Marta," he said. "Before you take that away—can you stay a minute?" His eyes flicked to the bathroom door.

Well, Marta said to herself. *He lost his shyness quickly enough.*

"I think I can do it without the chair," he said, swinging his legs from under the blanket. "I feel much stronger today, but I'll still need your help."

His legs were shaky, but he managed to stand, holding on to Marta's chair. She had one hand against his side for support, and she could feel his muscles working beneath her fingers. His hand on the back of her chair kept brushing her shoulder, and when she realized that he shifted to keep it there, a shiver passed through her. She had a sudden flashback to the night Dominic had kissed her for the first time.

She had been sitting on the edge of the pier. Be careful, Dominic had said. He was worried about her falling. But she was out of her chair, and the last thing she was worried about was falling—she felt like she was flying, instead. She'd felt secure in his arms. And exhilarated. Her fingers had felt the strength of his muscles then too as she clung to him. When he'd kissed her, she suddenly *was* afraid of falling. Falling in love.

Marta shook off the memory. Because right after the kiss—right after the flying—had come the real fall. When Dominic told her who he was, that he had been the one who shot her, she'd wanted to fall right off the face of the earth.

Marta shrugged his hand from her shoulder as they reached the bathroom. They struggled to squeeze through the bathroom door together, and Dominic tripped, almost falling into her lap. He laughed as she reached to help hold him up, and at the sound of his laughter Marta froze. Mechanically she moved to give him access to the toilet, and wheeled herself backward out of the bathroom.

His laughter. In that laughter, Marta had heard something that chilled her, that reminded her of things she wished weren't true. The laugh was the laughter of happiness. It was also the laughter of relief. Dominic was recovering. He was walking. Soon he would be completely healed. And Marta was furious. Humiliated. Resentful.

Why was he getting better? He was going to be fine, while she . . . Well, she would never be "fine" again.

Marta sucked in her breath. It frightened her to realize what she was feeling. Had she wanted him to die? No, she knew that she had never wanted that. But something else. She wanted him to suffer. It was as simple as that. She wanted justice. No excuses. No explanations. No time off for good behavior or changing his life.

She never realized how much anger she still carried inside her for the shooting. She thought she'd put it in the past, until the past had come to confront her. Now she knew her own anger. Her resentment. It was thick enough to fill her throat so that she could barely breathe. She would choke on it if she let herself.

Dominic was going to walk. He was going to get up from it all, from everything, his past and her suffering, and stroll away a free man.

The bathroom door opened, and Dominic stood uneasily in the doorway, leaning against the jamb, waiting for her to come and help him. But when he caught her eye, and saw the expression on her face, he turned pale.

"Marta?" he asked tentatively. "What's wrong? What have I done?" His voice was desperate, but she didn't care.

"What do you mean, what have you done?" Marta shouted. "How can you ask me that? Look at you. You're walking! Your suffering is ending. It's already over! But mine—"

"Marta!" Dominic cried. "Marta, please—"

"—will go on and on. Forever!"

"What can I do?" Dominic pleaded.

Marta heard him, and watched him slide to the floor. Then she rolled over and helped pull him up. He was crying as she led him wordlessly back to the bed. Then she turned away and left the room.

She had no answer to give him.

Kate sat straight in her lifeguarding chair—her elbows on the armrests, her hand lightly touching a pair of binoculars resting against her thigh. She had on her red cap, her sunglasses, and a thin smear of zinc oxide on her nose. There was a good breeze today, and the sky was cloudless and pure blue. It wasn't as hot as usual, but Kate knew that only meant more people would get fried today because they wouldn't be wearing sunscreen. People never seemed to realize that as long as it was clear, the rays would get them anyway, whether it was sixty-five degrees or ninety.

Kate stopped scanning the water long enough to give a careful look up and down the beach. It was a mildly crowded Tuesday morning. Mostly young families in her section, and that meant a lot of little kids and babies. Kate could relax a little on that score. Most of the little kids wouldn't even get near the water, and all lifeguards knew that mommies were the second-best defense against carelessness.

They usually stood in a line, five or six across, water up to their knees, arms crossed while gossiping, their heads scanning back and forth in a row like a squadron of professionally trained lifeguards. They constantly kept track of each other's children, calling out sharply to young boys roughhousing on boogie boards and girls arguing over floats. Sometimes it was hard to tell which kids belonged to which mothers. When it came to the beach, there seemed an unspoken agreement among parents. All kids were fair game, and it was a mother's job to yell at them and make sure they were safe.

Then Kate saw Justin walking toward her across the sand, and her heart skipped a beat. He looked as handsome as ever, barefoot and wearing nothing but an old pair of running shorts. He was carrying running shoes in his hand, and Kate guessed that he had just finished a boardwalk workout.

Kate turned back to the water, though she didn't really need to be so attentive. It gave her an excuse not to have to look at Justin.

"Kate," Justin said, coming to a stop beside her chair. "Nice day," he commented, nodding at the smattering of families on the beach.

"Yeah," she agreed, her head moving determinedly back and forth in its familiar pattern.

"I wanted to talk before I left," Justin explained.

"Before you left?"

"Last night, remember? I told you that I was going to get my boat."

"Oh, right." Kate nodded uncomfortably. The other woman.

"David's friend is taking me to the Bahamas. That's where the boat is now," Justin said.

"When are you leaving?" Kate asked, her mouth suddenly dry.

"Tomorrow," she heard him say, and it was like a clamp closing down on her heart.

"I doubt I'll get back to O.C. until the end of the summer, and I just didn't feel right about leaving without trying to . . . resolve things between us." Justin struggled for words.

"What about Marta?" Kate asked.

"Marta's great. It's important to have a friend who can understand why you hurt," Justin explained. "We both have this similar problem." Justin winced. "We're in love with other people."

"People?" Kate asked, barely breathing.

"Yes," Justin said. "This woman I'm in love with, you know her well. She's the one who says I have no future with her. And I guess she's right. It's just hard to admit, and I wanted to hear her explain it one more time. To make sure I understand."

Kate nodded. "She has to go to college," she said, trying not to hear his words in her head, *this woman I'm in love with.* "And she has plans for her life. Things she wants to accomplish. A career."

"And I don't," Justin said. "Not beyond getting back to my boat and sailing the world. But if she were as smart as she claims, she'd understand that seeing life, experiencing it, is the best kind of education there is."

"For some," Kate said sadly. "Perhaps in your travels you'll realize that there *are* issues worth devoting your life to beyond your own personal freedom."

"Like what?" Justin asked.

"People," Kate responded.

"I'm a person," Justin said softly.

Kate caught her breath. "I know," she whispered.

Justin sighed and ran a hand through his hair.

"And I wanted to tell you how sorry I am," he continued. "About what happened with Tosh."

Kate winced, and wished Justin would stop speaking. All she could think about was that day on the dock when she'd chosen Tosh so vehemently. When she'd defended him and claimed he shared her principles. Some principles!

"He was a fool," Justin said, and Kate's head snapped up. "Any guy who would treat you that way is a fool."

Justin turned to look at her, and Kate couldn't help looking back. His eyes were beautiful. His smile sad. She felt the lump in her throat and hoped he would go away before she started sobbing.

"Anyone who would let you get away," Justin went on, "is a fool. And he'll end up spending the rest of his life sailing around the world alone."

Kate turned back to the water, though she could no longer see it through her tears. She felt Justin reach up and touch her tenderly on the shoulder. She wanted to turn to him, to grab him and not let him go. To tell him she loved him.

But he was already leaving. Tomorrow. There wasn't time for anything anyway.

"Bye, Kate," Justin said.

"Good-bye," she whispered back.

FOURTEEN

Connor bought a pretzel from a vendor and rubbed away most of the salt before tearing off a piece and popping it in his mouth. He chewed slowly and nodded to himself, formulating his new plan.

Last night hadn't gone any better with Chelsea than the night before. True, they'd worked well together. And somehow their sniping seemed to help fuel their creativity. But on the reconciliation front, things could be considered a total disaster. As much as he couldn't believe she wasn't softening to him, Connor had to be impressed. She was sticking to her word. Not like him. He was ready to get on his knees and beg.

He knew not telling his parents that Chelsea was black hadn't been the best thing to do. But she didn't know his parents. And it was true that in cases like this, simple words, like, *Mum, I married a black woman and she's okay*, wouldn't change generations of ingrained belief. His parents weren't racist. Connor knew that. They were just sheltered, and there was a world of difference, even if Chelsea didn't want to admit it.

Ah, his parents. They were arriving tomorrow, and Connor and Chelsea were no closer to getting back together than they'd been last week. He hated to think that his parents wouldn't meet her. While Chelsea seemed to think the big shock would be that she was black, the truth was that his parents would die of heartbreak if they knew he and his wife were separated.

He was their only son, and he knew they loved him. Probably too much for their own good. Ah, they spoiled him, that was the problem. That was why he hated disappointing them. Why he ended up lying, or saying nothing, instead. He knew how much it would hurt them if he didn't show up at the airport with a wife. And although Connor knew it was pretty bad form, he was trying to find one, at least for the weekend.

He was on the boardwalk, looking intently at every woman who passed. How ridiculous would it be, he thought, to go up and ask a complete stranger, 'Excuse me, will you be my wife for five days?' He was willing to pay, too. And it would only be for show. For the meet and greet, and walk and talk. Nothing in the bedroom. Just a regular working day. Well, a regular day plus overtime.

There! That one seemed polite. Straight brown hair. Pretty enough, but not too beautiful. Neat looking. Could he ask her? Would she laugh in his face?

"Ah, excuse me, miss," Connor said, stepping in front of her. "May I talk to you for a moment?"

"Um." The girl squinted up at him. "Do I know you?" she asked.

Connor cringed a little. Her voice was sharp and a bit piercing. "Well, actually, no you don't," he explained. "Connor's the name. And yours?"

"Joyce," she answered, her voice like fingernails on a chalkboard. "What do you want? Are you picking me up? I like your accent."

"I have a proposition for you, not that way, and thank you," Connor replied to all her questions.

"Huh?"

"Well." He smiled. "I'm looking for a wife. As a business arrangement—"

"A wife?" she screeched.

Connor shivered. Joyce the Voice was too

much for him already. But she seemed hooked on the idea, and curious. How could he get away now? He looked up and saw his escape route walking away from him along the boardwalk. Grace! Ah, a much better plan.

"Yes!" Connor cried, grabbing Joyce by the arms and kissing her cheek. "Thank you! My wife, I was looking for my wife, and there she is. I see her. Thanks so much. Pleasure meeting you!" he cried as he moved away into the crowd.

"Grace," Connor yelled out desperately, sprinting up the boardwalk to catch her.

"My hero," Grace teased. "How are you? You look terrible."

"Can we sit a moment, Grace?" Connor begged. "I've got a very important favor to ask you."

They found an open table with an umbrella, and Connor sank down into a chair. He was still breathing hard from his run. *Poet, not athlete,* he reminded his ego when he caught sight of Grace's laughing eyes.

"What can I do for you?" she asked curiously.

"I need a wife while my parents are here," Connor blurted out. "I know it sounds crazy," he rushed on, holding up a hand to quiet her, "but Chelsea refuses to meet them. She's mad at me for a number of reasons which I won't enumerate at the moment, boring story that it is, and the result, of course, is that I have no wife to introduce to my parents when they arrive tomorrow."

Connor took a deep breath.

"So I need a replacement. A stand-in. I promise I won't try anything funny, although it would be nice if you let me kiss you once or twice in front of them. On the cheek is fine," Connor hastened to say.

"Can I get you anything?" the waitress asked, appearing at his side.

"Too early for a beer?" Connor asked, checking his watch. "Yes, perhaps it is. Large glass of water for me, thanks. Grace?" he asked.

She shook her head.

"Oh, then, make that two waters for me," Connor said. "Is that okay? We'll only sit for a minute. I promise."

The waitress huffed, put her pad away, and stalked off.

"Do you think she's going to bring that water?" Connor asked. "I really am thirsty. And it's hot out."

"It's cool," Grace said. "There's a breeze; you're just out of shape."

"Okay, then, no kisses. I'll come up with some excuse." Connor smiled. "I'll tell them you're shy, how's that?"

"Now, Connor, wait—" Grace began to laugh. "You don't need to explain anymore. Let me ask you a question, though. Do you really think I can pass for Chelsea? I mean, I have an all-right tan for this time of year, but . . ."

"Well," Connor admitted. "That's one of the things Chelsea's mad at me about." He paused and looked away for a minute. "Unfortunately, my parents don't actually know that she's black."

"They don't know?"

"I know, I know," Connor said, wincing. "Believe me, I've already heard everything you could possibly say to me."

"Including that you're a jerk?" Grace asked skeptically.

"That's kid's stuff," Connor replied.

"Well, listen, Connor," Grace explained. "I'm actually almost amused by the idea. And although I might, and I stress *might*, have been convinced to help you out, I'm actually going away tomorrow. I'm sorry, Connor," Grace said, smiling sweetly. "Maybe you should try your real wife one more time?"

That was easy for Grace to say, Connor thought as he stalked off down the boardwalk. Who could he ask now? Marta? No, she didn't seem like the lie-for-you type.

Then he saw a familiar figure coming out of Floater's—Kate, on her way back to her lifeguarding chair. Connor shrugged. She'd probably say no, but what was the harm in asking?

*   *   *

Later Connor laughed at his own question.

Kate looked almost ready to kill him when he broached the subject of her being his stand-in wife.

"Chelsea said you sometimes acted like a child—but you're not really this dumb, are you?" she asked in disbelief.

"Chelsea called me a child?" he muttered.

"How did you ever convince yourself that it was worth asking me this?" Kate marveled. "What went on in that tiny brain of yours?"

"I figured you might say no—"

"I *might* say no?" Kate gasped. "I'm Chelsea's best friend! You can't possibly believe that I would do that to her!"

"I guess not," he sighed. "No harm in asking, though. I don't feel comfortable asking a stranger—"

"You're going to ask someone else?" Kate shrieked. "Someone you don't even know?"

She was carrying a life preserver under her arm, and Connor wondered for a brief moment if one had ever been used as a dangerous weapon. She looked like she wanted to clock him over the head with it. Or strangle him.

"Connor," she said before stalking away, "it isn't really my business how you and Chelsea solve your problems, but do me a favor—don't come swimming near me for a while. As a lifeguard, I've never drowned anyone before, but you might inspire me to try it."

After that Connor didn't dare ask anyone else, and so he went home to tackle the cleanliness problem. Since it would have to pass as an acceptable stand-in for a wife, Connor wanted to clean the dump up. No, Mum, he imagined himself saying, no wife. But look, a great little balcony, *and* a view of the ocean. See? If you lean over and wrap yourself around the edge, just like that . . .

In his effort to clean the apartment, he'd already vacuumed the living room, although most of Mooch's dog hair seemed permanently attached to the carpeting. He'd tried to mop the kitchen floor, but he didn't have a mop, so he ended up sponging it clean on his hands and knees. For the past twenty minutes, he'd been working on the coffee table with ammonia and a fork, but still, the strange sticky residue wouldn't come off. There was a knock on the door, and Connor gladly laid down the fork. Interruption was a good reason to quit.

He opened the door, and Bo stepped in.

"Justin around?" he asked.

"Nah," Connor replied. "Sorry, just the cleaning lady."

"I thought it looked different in here," Bo said, taking a cursory look around. "What are you cleaning for?"

"My parents are coming."

"From Ireland?" Bo seemed impressed.

"Yup. And I need to have a nice apartment, seeing as how I'll be lacking a nice wife," he muttered. "Stay away from women, Bo," Connor exclaimed suddenly.

"Why?" Bo asked.

"They'll ruin your life," Connor moaned. "Just take a look at me. Dishpan hands!" Connor thrust his hands out in front of him. "And I'm doing this because my own wife refuses to meet my parents. You see the spot they can put you in?" Connor asked.

"Sure," Bo said, staring at Connor.

"It's power, Bo," Connor hissed. "Look what they can reduce a man to. Ashes. And do you know why?"

Bo shook his head.

"Because they like it, the witches. And do you know how?"

Bo shook his head again.

"She'll make you weak. That's how. Because you'll find yourself near her, and you won't be able to breathe. She's like an infection that crawls inside your head and gives you a fever."

Connor walked toward him, and Bo started

backing away slowly to the door.

"All you'll want to do is love her, but she'll yell at you and complain. You'll forget to go to the store, just once, for some milk, or cat food, or garbage bags, it won't matter what exactly, and you'll come home to a demon with wild hair who'll sprinkle dead bugs in your bed."

Bo's back was against the door, his mouth open.

"She'll use the same name as the woman you fell in love with," Connor ranted, "but she'll say terrible things to you. Take all your secrets and throw them back in your face so you can't hide. Insecure. Shamed. Jealous. And then—" Connor paused dramatically. "And then, she'll leave you. And thrive. And you'll watch from a distance, like a stranger, while she does everything she said she would do. Leaving you behind."

Connor moaned to himself. Chelsea, Chelsea, Chelsea—he missed her so much.

"The problem is, Bo, that we deserve it all," Connor said. "Men aren't good enough for women. As soon as you start believing they are, it's over. You've lost."

Bo quickly opened the door behind him and stood still, lingering in the doorway, unable to leave.

"This is my advice," Connor said sadly. "If you ever find true love, thank the Lord, and do everything she tells you to. Just don't let her go."

Connor hardly heard the door when it closed. He sank into a chair and dropped his head into his hands in his cleaner, emptier, and lonelier apartment.

FIFTEEN

In the darkness, Marta listened to the steady breathing from the bed nearby. Dominic was asleep. After their confrontation that morning, Marta had left him alone for the rest of the day, except to bring a tray of food for lunch and dinner. She didn't trust herself to be with him. To see him feeling good.

She had been thinking all day about what he had asked her. She was still trying to come up with an answer.

What *could* he do?

Nothing. That was the answer to that.

But there was another question: What could *she* do? That was the question keeping her awake.

It wasn't a simple choice between forgiving him or not. The problem was, Marta didn't know if she could forgive him, even if it turned out she wanted to.

She kept asking herself what she could do, but the only answer she got was a voice that kept reminding her: *What did he do? What did he do?*

Look what he did! she wanted to scream. *Look what he did to me!* The anger was there, pulsing below her surface. Marta could call it up so quickly that it frightened her. Was she to be that kind of person, then? Angry all her life?

Justin had called her sneaky. Determined, she had replied. And he agreed. He admired her for that determination. But was this admirable, what she was doing? And was it fair? Life had been unfair to her. It had. She needed to admit it now. She had been resenting that for so long, pretending that she didn't care. You can't live your life only according to what is fair and unfair, she used to say. You have to take responsibility sometime.

How easy those things had been to say, Marta realized. She never imagined that living them would be so hard.

Chelsea threw her sketch pad across her room and snapped off the light beside her bed. Another productive evening of work at the condo, and a complete failure of communication.

She and Connor hadn't spoken about his parents. Chelsea was determined not to ask him any personal questions. She'd wanted a professional relationship and she was getting one. But Connor had been much more reserved tonight.

There had been no sparring. No quips. And without those things, she felt the distance between them grow.

She was still angry at him. She couldn't believe that he had tried to make up with her for the sake of his parents. Didn't he care at all how she might be feeling? That for her there were more important things than what his parents might think? It was all appearances for him. A big show.

It hurt her to think that it had all been for his parents, that he hadn't been happy for himself to have her back.

But maybe he had been. And maybe it was the selfish reason, his parents' visit, that had forced him to do something about it. That was the trouble with Connor, Chelsea thought with a sigh. You never knew exactly why he did what he did. He wasn't one for admitting his true feelings. So his actions had to be judged on the surface. And on the surface, he was behaving like a creep.

Chelsea sat up and pulled her covers around her. Of course, she admitted, Connor had never claimed to be a saint. He'd warned her enough about that before they were married. But she had always believed that there was a core of goodness inside him. She knew there was, it was just that sometimes it was hard to see.

Chelsea pounded her pillow and leaned back against the wall. How could he not have told his parents that she was black! Didn't he understand at all how humiliated that made her feel?

Well, he didn't have to be embarrassed. Or worried. Because his parents were never going to meet her. And he wouldn't have to explain anything ever again.

Bo was dying.

It felt like he was dying.

Maybe he should take a shower. That's what guys were supposed to do when they felt this way. A cold shower.

Bo shivered. It seemed too harsh.

Maybe some Maalox? He needed something for his stomach. It was growling, but he knew he wasn't hungry.

He was in love.

He couldn't possibly go to sleep, not with Roan in the same house. He couldn't stop thinking of Roan, downstairs in her room, curled up on the cot. She was so close.

Bo sighed. Holding hands. Boy, that had been a tough one. He knew she was worried about doing everything right. It was important for him, too. He really wanted this relationship to work. Roan was the first girl he'd ever felt this way about.

He smiled to himself. She was perfect, wonderful, funny, pretty. And she was still tough, no doubt about that. But even though he was dying of frustration, he was happy about the way things were. He liked her even more now. So he was all for doing things the right way.

Bo was ready to be a gentleman. Even if it was hard. Especially now. When he was awake. When he knew where she was, how close she was. He smiled and closed his eyes. Well, at least he wouldn't have to wait that long to see her again. He knew where she'd be for breakfast.

Grace went out onto the deck. Her nightgown pressed against her in the cool midnight breeze. The ocean was a slow and steady hum against the beach, and the night sky was full of stars. Grace imagined that she was the only one in the world awake at this moment. Surely the only one in the house.

She sighed and wrapped her arms tightly around her stomach. She was nervous, and she couldn't sleep. This was going to be another journey. Last summer, she'd gone to New York City with Chelsea and Kate. Then she'd spent seven months sailing across the ocean with Justin.

So why was one little day-trip to Macon, Georgia, scaring her so much?

Because she was going to ask Roan's mother, a stranger, to let someone else take care of her daughter.

Perhaps Roan's mother wasn't mean, just weak, or tired, or sad. In any case, Grace didn't have too much room for sympathy or pity. Roan needed stability, and Grace wanted to offer it. She could afford to offer it; so shouldn't she?

Grace had the money. She had the room. She shared the history. And Grace did have sympathy for Roan. She liked Roan, too. Even before, when she'd been an insolent and tough-talking smart-ass. Grace respected anyone who gave her a run for her money in the quick-and-witty put-down department. She liked Roan more, now that she was trying to straighten herself out.

Grace turned and went back into her bedroom. She sat on the bed carefully and watched David sleep. He was why she could do what she was doing tomorrow. Grace knew how lucky she was to have David standing by her.

She reached out and pushed his hair from his face, and he made a small noise in his sleep. He looked so peaceful that at first Grace didn't want to wake him. Then she just couldn't help herself. She was nervous, and she wanted him to hold her, to be with her, to tell her again how she was doing the right thing. She leaned over and began kissing him. She kissed him until he murmured, and his eyelids fluttered open in the darkness.

"I'm sorry to wake you," Grace said softly, resting her head on his chest.

"What's wrong?" David asked groggily.

"Nothing," Grace said. "Nothing at all. I missed you."

David smiled and opened his arms for her. Grace slipped under the blankets and cuddled against him, and he tightened his arm around her.

"Don't worry," he said, with that uncanny ability he had to read her mind. "You'll be fine tomorrow. Everything will work out. You're doing the right thing, Grace," he whispered.

"You really think so?" she asked.

"Are you questioning me?" He chuckled. "You could get punished for that, you know."

"I could?" Grace asked, snuggling closer. "Well, tell me what kind of punishment I get, and then I'll decide if I'm guilty or not."

"It starts off something like this," he whispered, taking her head in his hands and lowering his mouth to hers. He kissed her softly and sweetly. Grace sighed into his mouth. "But it gets worse."

"How much worse?" Grace asked, her eyes closed.

"How guilty are you?"

"I think I'm very, very guilty." Grace smiled.

"Maximum sentence?" David suggested, biting her earlobe.

"Mmm," Grace agreed.

"That could last all night, you know."

"I hope so," she said, pulling him down to her.

The boardwalk was deserted. The shops closed and shuttered. The beach empty. The water seemed to be the only moving surface. Justin leaned against the rail, faintly illuminated by the light from the stars shining in the black cloudless sky. The lifeguard chairs stood tall and vacant, like sentries in the sand, watching the ocean. He would be leaving tomorrow to begin another journey.

He remembered how he felt at the end of last summer—in the days before he was about to leave, he had been sorry that Kate wasn't going with him. He had been hurt, and disappointed. But still, there was the excitement of the trip. It had been an excitement he couldn't contain, a power that had overtaken his sadness for Kate. Leaving her had been hard, but the sea had called to him, and had managed to make up for her absence somehow.

But this time Justin knew it was different, and it frightened him. The sea was still there, the excitement, the freedom of his boat. But it wasn't enough this time. It didn't feel like enough. His loneliness was stronger. He wanted Kate to be with him.

Then he heard the soft scratching sound of shoes on the boardwalk, and his heart started beating louder.

Kate saw him staring at the sea. She knew that he had heard her, and she stopped. She had been drawn out tonight, and she didn't know why. She had just been restless—she couldn't bear lying in her bed any longer, feeling powerless and alone. She knew it had to do with what Justin had said to her earlier. First, that he still loved her. And second, that he was leaving her again.

She had gone for a walk, thinking that she would be alone. That she would have all of Ocean City to herself to remember each moment they had spent together there. She knew everything would look different tomorrow, after he left, and she wanted to get a last look at how it had been before.

Looking back, Kate could see that they had been doomed from the start. They had both seemed to know that it could never work between them. Still, they struggled through two summers together. If they started again now, it would end the same way, because nothing had changed. The rest of their lives, the way they each wanted to live, could not be made to fit, no matter how good they were together. No matter how Justin made her feel when he kissed her. There would always be later. The next day. The next year. The future.

Kate sighed deeply. The future was tomorrow. Tomorrow Justin was leaving again. She thought fleetingly that she should turn, walk away, walk back to the safety of the house, and climb into bed and try to begin to get along without him. But her body wasn't listening. Her feet continued to carry her toward him.

"Kate," he said. He was still staring at the ocean.

She moved up beside him and looked where he was looking.

"What do you see?" she asked quietly.

"I'm looking at a dream," he said wistfully, "of you and me on a boat together, floating aimlessly on the waves. Enjoying the sun. Enjoying each other."

"You can't be aimless forever," Kate said sadly.

"For a little while," he replied.

"For tonight?" she asked softly, turning to him.

They reached for each other blindly and desperately. He kissed her, and she lost her grip on time.

"I have to go," Justin said, holding her tightly.

"I know," she sighed.

"You'll be gone by the time I come back here," he went on. "If I come back here."

"Where will you go?" she asked.

"I don't know," Justin answered. "I can't keep coming back to Ocean City. It's part of what you say. I don't have my future planned, but it's beginning to take shape somewhere in my mind, and it isn't here. At least if I'm not with you. It will make me crazy, all this remembering."

Kate nodded. "I won't come back again either," she admitted. "I don't think I can. I realized that when we talked today. It hurts too much."

"I never wanted to hurt you—" Justin began.

"I know," Kate said.

"—but I also never thought I would hurt so much," he ended simply, sadly.

"I'm sorry," Kate said, "I wish there was another way—"

Justin stopped her with a kiss. It was no use imagining something that neither of them could have. Kate couldn't conceive of a life without college—without the future she wanted so much for herself. She knew Justin could never give up the sea. Asking him to stay home was like trying to keep a dolphin in a bathtub for a pet. There just wasn't enough room to swim.

They had tried. More than once, but there

wasn't a way, or they would have found it. And if they gave up too much of themselves, they wouldn't be happy. Even together.

Justin bent over and picked Kate up in his arms as he stepped off the boardwalk onto the sand. Kate hardly felt it when he placed her on the beach. All she cared about was that she not lose contact, not for a second, with him on their last night together.

Because it was their last night.

"I love you, Kate," Justin whispered in her ear as she melted into his embrace.

SIXTEEN

Chelsea had a long day to kill before she met Connor in the afternoon. She figured she'd hang out on the boardwalk and do some sketching. She would just grab a banana or something before she left. She stepped into the kitchen and ran straight into Dominic.

"Aaah!" they shrieked at the same time.

"This is a dangerous corner," Chelsea said when she'd caught her breath and her heartbeat was back to normal. "A high-traffic area. Maybe we should get a yield sign." He didn't respond to her joke. "By the way, are you all right? Are you supposed to be out of bed? Should I call Marta at the clinic?"

"No, please!" Dominic cried. He sat down quickly. "Really," he said, "I'm fine. I was just looking for the yellow pages."

"Let your fingers do the walking, huh?" Chelsea joked.

Dominic looked at her.

"Sorry," she said wryly, "but it has been claimed by some that I have a pretty *good* sense of humor."

Dominic smiled. "Listen, Chelsea, I'm trying to get my hands on something. Maybe you'll be able to help."

"Tell me what you want. I'm on my way out, actually, but I'll be home in a few hours."

"Well," Dominic said with a strange expression on his face, "I need a video camera, actually."

"Home movies?" Chelsea joked. "Baby's first steps and all that?"

"No," he said vaguely. "It's just something I need. For myself."

Chelsea wondered what he could possibly want with a camera, but figured it wasn't her business to ask. Besides, he was acting pretty cloak-and-dagger about the whole thing.

"I think I actually can get you one of those. For free. I used to work for this beach-photography place in town. You know, love-in-the-surf portrait shots and whatnot." Chelsea winked. "Anyway, I'll stop by and see if they have a camera I can borrow. How long will you need it?"

"For an hour or so, I guess."

"All right," Chelsea said, shaking her head. "I'll see what I can do."

There was a strange odor coming from the kitchen, so Connor had his head under the kitchen sink. That was why it took a while before he finally realized that someone was banging on his door. Loudly.

"Can you get that!" he screeched, banging his head on a pipe. "Damn!"

Connor listened a moment and realized that the shower was on. That would be Justin, he thought, always busy when you needed him. Connor was disengaging himself from the plumbing when he heard the water in the shower turn off. Then the knocking at the door grew even louder.

He heard the sound of the bathroom door open and close, Justin muttering as he crossed the living room, and then the front door. And lots of loud talking.

"Connor!" Justin called. "Your folks are here!"

What! His parents! What were they doing here already? It was barely morning. He'd only been up half an hour. Connor panicked, pulled himself from the floor, took a deep breath, and went into the living room.

His parents were standing in the doorway, looking skeptically at Justin. Justin, on the other hand, wasn't exactly looking like the welcome wagon himself, wearing nothing but a damp towel around his waist.

"Connor?" his mom said shakily.

"Son." His father's voice was gruff.

"Is this where you live?" his father asked, looking quickly at Justin and then back at Connor.

Why are they looking at me like that? Connor wondered. Then Justin started giggling, and Connor looked down at himself. He was wearing his boxer shorts and an apron. The apron was for protection under the sink, he would explain. Then there was the matter of the toilet bowl scrubber he was clutching in his right hand. And the shower cap he had on his head.

"Um, plumbing," he said, turning beet red. "There was a smell—" He faltered, nodding behind him. "In the sink. I think."

"Why don't I check on that?" Justin suddenly said. Connor looked and saw a malicious glint in his eye.

Justin took hold of his towel with one hand, and in an exaggerated walk he sauntered over to Connor, took the scrubber from his hand, and patted him on the butt before disappearing into the kitchen.

Mrs. Riordan's eyes popped. And then she fainted to the floor. Connor went to his mother, who opened her eyes, took another look at him in his apron and boxer shorts, and fainted away again.

"Get back!" his father cried, watching Justin leave the kitchen and enter the bedroom. "Give her some room, and get dressed."

"I'll wait for him to come out," Connor said, nodding toward his room.

After a few minutes of deadly silence, Mr. Riordan looked over at Connor. "Don't get shy on account of us," he said. "You've already just about killed her. You couldn't do much worse."

"Da," Connor said, "it's not what you think."

Seconds later Justin emerged from Connor's room, fully clothed, with his knapsack on his shoulder, a huge metal cage under his arm, and a wicked grin on his face.

"What is that thing?" Mr. Riordan asked, looking at the cage. "Was that in your bedroom, son?" he asked, horrified.

"Yes, but Da, really, it's for the dog, okay?" Connor cried.

"Come on, Mooch," Justin called. Mooch barked and came from behind the couch, where he'd been cowering from the noise. "Time to go, boy," Justin said, scratching the dog behind the ears.

"Let me see you out," Connor replied with clenched teeth. "I hate you," he said as soon as they stepped outside.

"I'll write," Justin promised.

"I hope you drown," Connor snarled.

"You can't mean it," Justin said in mock terror. "Look, at least I'm giving you something to talk about. Now when you tell them that Chelsea is black, they'll be so happy, they'll kiss your feet."

"If they don't kill me first," Connor moaned.

"Take care." Justin squeezed his shoulder.

"You too," Connor said, offering a wry smile.

"Don't stand out here too long," Justin warned. "They're sure to think we're kissing."

Connor blushed and went back into the apartment.

One more thing to misinterpret.

"Aaahhh!" his mother wailed, seeing his red face.

This would be a very long visit.

"Is everyone set to go?" Peter Latham asked the crowd standing on the tarmac of the small airport. "Justin? You got all your gear stowed in the back? That hairy dog all comfortable?"

Justin nodded, and he, Grace, and David climbed into the small plane.

"You sure we'll make it all the way to the Bahamas in this?" Justin asked skeptically.

Peter laughed. It was a deep, comfortable sound. He scratched his beard. "We'll have to hop up and down a few times for gas, but we'll make it," he vowed, his eyes twinkling. "David," he said, turning to his old flying buddy, "you going to be my copilot for this first leg?"

"Sure am," David said, strapping himself into the seat next to Peter's.

"Where are you going again?" Justin asked Grace as she settled down beside him.

"Macon," Grace said nervously.

"What's there, Racey? What's the big secret?"

"If I tell you, do you promise that you won't think I'm crazy?" she asked.

"I promise," Justin agreed.

"Have you got everything you need from Gen?" David turned in his seat to ask Grace one more time before they left.

She nodded, and he gave her the thumbs-up and blew her a kiss.

"Who's Gen?" Justin asked.

"The lawyer," Grace replied.

"So?" Justin said curiously. "What's in Macon?" He broke a huge grin. "Are you guys getting married?"

Just then Peter started up the engine. Grace shook her head and laughed, pointing with her thumb at the roof of the plane, meaning, I'll tell you everything when we get up there.

"Say good-bye," Grace mouthed as she took Justin's hand and squeezed it.

Justin turned to look out the window as they took off. As soon as they were in the air, Peter banked in a long slow turn to the right, pointing the nose of the plane due south. Below him Justin could see the stretch of beach where he had spent so much of his life. Kate was down there now, and he wondered if she was thinking of him. He put his hand against the window. They had said good-bye last night. He couldn't bring himself to do it again.

The sound of the small-engine plane caught her attention. Kate knew even before she checked her watch that it was the plane Justin was on. She paused in her sweep of the ocean to make a quick search of the sky. And there it was. The plane passed over her in seconds.

Kate wrapped her arms around herself and shivered, though the sun was out. It was, in fact, a beautiful day, but she suddenly felt cold.

"Good-bye," she whispered softly to herself. "I'm sorry."

"Okay," Chelsea said that night in the condo. "I can't stand it anymore. I told myself I wouldn't ask you anything non-work-related, but this is ridiculous. What *have* you been up to all day? You look terrible!"

Connor sighed and shook his head. He was

sitting at the desk, exhausted and depressed.

"If this is some ploy . . ." Chelsea threatened. "If you're trying to make me feel bad . . ."

Connor shook his head.

"All right, give it up. What happened?"

"Well, my parents arrived a little earlier than expected," he began. "I wasn't quite prepared. And anyway, I had this whole plan for how I was going to sit them down and explain to them why they wouldn't be meeting you—"

"A plan?" Chelsea snorted. "You mean you had a good lie ready?"

"No, really. The truth. But I wanted to tell them myself. You know, why I hadn't told them before. But anyway, they got there early, and Justin was getting out of the shower, and I'd been cleaning up in the kitchen, and . . . I can't really explain it. . . . They just jumped to the completely wrong conclusion."

"You mean they thought . . . Justin was your . . . ?"

"Exactly," Connor said.

Chelsea burst out laughing.

"Don't laugh. You weren't the one who had to spend the rest of the day with them."

"Why?" Chelsea asked, trying to control her giggles.

"Because the first thing we did was go to the travel agent. They're leaving tomorrow."

"Oh, Connor," Chelsea said, suddenly serious. "I'm sorry."

Connor shrugged. "Well, at this point I can't blame them. I don't really want them to stay either. I spent the day showing them around town, trying to convince them I wasn't gay, but it didn't matter. 'There's the ocean,' I said, 'and I'm not gay. There's the amusement park,' I said, 'and I have a wife. This is where I had my first illegal job,' I said, and her name's Chelsea, just like I wrote you.'"

"So?" Chelsea asked. "They didn't crack?"

"My father isn't even speaking to me anymore," Connor moaned. "Do you know what that means in an Irish family, when your own father won't say your name? It's terrible, is what it is. Terrible. 'Tell that . . . person,' my father says to my mum—he can't even bring himself to call me his son. 'Tell that person,' he says to her. 'Tell him I need a drink.' And my mum turns to me, good wife that she is—'Connor, son, your father needs a—' 'I heard him myself,' I say. 'He needs a drink. So do I!'"

Chelsea couldn't help herself. It was terrible, really, but it was also funny. A part of her wanted to say it served him right, but she didn't dare.

"Chels," Connor sighed. "Can I ask you something?"

"What?"

"After my parents leave," he said, looking up

at her, his eyes earnest and sincere, "do you think that we could try again . . . to put things right between us?"

"After?" Chelsea echoed.

"Because I really love you," Connor said. "I want you to know that. And I missed you today. Not only because it would have been easier. Maybe it wouldn't, I don't know. Just because— I'm tired of being without you," he said softly.

Chelsea smiled. She had to admit she was pleasantly surprised. If all Connor wanted from her was a wife to show his parents, he'd be pushing for them to get back together now. Not that Chelsea didn't think Connor was capable of that kind of manipulation—she knew he was. But it was a nice change to realize that he wasn't trying it with her. A definite step in the right direction.

And it never had been a question of love, Chelsea could admit. She had always loved Connor, and she knew he had loved her, as well. But loving each other wasn't all there was to it. They needed to learn how to live together.

"What time tomorrow?" she asked.

"They leave tomorrow at three o'clock. How about three thirty?" he asked, his eyes shining.

"Where do you want me?" Chelsea asked.

Connor nodded behind her at the bed.

Chelsea laughed, and punched him on the arm.

SEVENTEEN

David pulled the rental car over to the curb. It had taken them a while at the county clerk's office to locate Roan's mother. Then they'd gotten lost trying to find her house. But finally they'd found the shabby home on a parched piece of grass in a run-down neighborhood outside of Macon.

David turned off the engine and reached for Grace's hand.

"Are you ready?" he asked.

She nodded.

"You've already done a great thing coming this far, you know," David said. "Be prepared if it doesn't work. She might not be ready for someone like you." David looked at her in her carefully chosen cream linen suit. "You might intimidate her," he said. "Whatever you do, don't lose your temper."

"I won't." Grace nodded, her throat tight.

"Ready?"

"Let's go," Grace said, opening the car door and swinging her legs out.

They walked to the door and knocked. Grace could hear a TV on inside. A muffled shout. Then the curtain in the picture window parted quickly and dropped back into place. The locks turned. The door swung open, and Grace found herself looking at a striking version of Roan. It was easy to see that the woman was beautiful, or had been not so long ago, with the same large doelike brown eyes. She was Roan twenty years older, after a long hard life.

"Ms. Prentice?" Grace asked, her voice shaky.

"Who's asking?" she replied.

"My name is Grace Caywood," Grace said, offering her hand. She dropped it after a moment and gestured instead to David. "This is my friend, David Jacobs."

"What do you want?" Roan's mother asked, looking her carefully up and down.

"I wonder if I might come in for a minute," Grace asked. "It's about your daughter, Roan. I'd like to talk to you about her."

At the mention of Roan's name, her mother's eyes grew scared, and the toughness went out of her body. She stood before them, clutching her dress, afraid.

"Is she all right?" her mother asked. "She's not—"

"No, ma'am," David said quickly, stepping forward and touching her arm. "She's fine. She's living with Grace right now. That's what we'd like to talk about."

"Okay, okay," Roan's mother said, moving aside for them. "Please, come in. And call me Anne," she said.

"Okay, Anne." Grace smiled. "Thanks very much for seeing us."

Anne brought them into the living room, where a rough-looking man with black hair and hard eyes was watching television.

"This is my husband, Lyle," Anne said to Grace and David. "Lyle, please, turn off the television for a minute, won't you? These people are here to talk about Roan."

Grace saw that Lyle immediately stiffened. His eyes darted around the room, almost afraid.

"Are you the police?" he demanded.

"No," Grace said quickly, wondering what he had to hide from the police. She didn't care, didn't want to know.

As quickly and clearly as she could, Grace outlined her conversation with the lawyer, explaining what the legal ramifications were of the custody transfer. Basically, that Grace would be Roan's legal guardian for two more years, until she was eighteen.

"You want to take her from me?" Anne asked when Grace was finished.

Grace quickly shook her head. "No, not at all. But let's be honest, Ms. Prentice. Roan isn't living with you anymore. According to the law, she's a runaway. If she ever got in trouble, got caught stealing from a drugstore, for example, she'd immediately be put in a juvenile detention center. Or at the very least, she would be turned over to the Protective Family Services, which might mean a string of foster homes. All I'm doing is offering to take care of her. To let her live with me, where she is now," Grace reminded them.

"What are you offering us?" Lyle asked, looking carefully at Grace's suit and bag and jewelry.

"Offering you?" Grace asked.

"Do you mean money?" David said.

"I don't mean anything," Lyle said vaguely. "I'm only asking the question."

"If you do mean money," Grace said, "I'm sorry, but I'm not offering anything. I don't want to buy Roan," she said tightly. "I want to help her. This isn't for you; it's for Roan."

"And what does Roan deserve?" Lyle said sharply. "I'll tell you what she deserves. A kick in the ass and a smack in the head. Look at the way she deserted her mother. And you want to take care of her? What for? You fall in love with

211

her?" he asked David. "You fall under her little spell? She's a teaser all right, our little Roan, she doesn't need your money—"

"Don't speak like that about her!" Anne cried.

"You see that?" Lyle said, shaking his finger. "You see how just the idea of that girl upsets her mother. If Roan wants a mother, the girl can come home," he said.

Grace took a breath to control herself. "That's right," she said carefully. "She can. But I don't think that's all she wants. And I don't think that's all she needs now. I'm not offering myself as a mother," Grace said, turning to Anne. "I'm offering her a friend. A legal home. A place where she wants to stay. Health insurance. Public school. You know she can't even go to school now, as a runaway. I'm offering another chance," Grace cried, her voice rising with her emotions.

"I say no!" Lyle exploded. "That girl was a pain in the ass. A bad seed. A no-good child. Always puttin' on airs. Who does she think she is, anyway? Who do you think *you* are!"

"Anne, please," Grace said, reaching for the woman's hands.

"Get out!" Lyle yelled. "Do you hear me? I don't need any lectures from you, girly. Roan wants to leave this house, well then, she's on her own, as far as her mother and I are concerned. That girl needs to be punished, not pampered.

212

That's her whole problem. Too damn spoiled. And that's your problem too, girly, you're too damn rich!"

"Come on, Grace," David said quickly, grabbing her by the arm. "Time to go." He pulled her up and took her bag and coat. Grace looked back over her shoulder as he led her from the room.

"Anne—" she begged. "Please—"

"*Out!*" the voice thundered.

Grace and David stumbled onto the small porch, and the door slammed shut behind them. Then they hurried across the street and got into their car.

"Grace," David said, turning to her. "Grace? It doesn't matter. She'll stay with you anyway. You can still take care of her. You can still help her."

Grace was shaking with anger, and tears were rolling down her cheeks. "He's terrible," she breathed. "Terrible. Poor Roan. But her mother . . . I don't understand. . . . Doesn't she care? Doesn't she see?"

David took her in his arms.

"It's not her fault, Grace," he said, trying to soothe her. "She's not a bad person. She's just overpowered. Maybe someday she'll get her act together and . . ." David let the sentence drift.

Grace sat up and wiped her face.

"Well, I'm glad we didn't tell Roan anything," she said sadly. "Let's get out of here."

David started the car up and put it in gear. He was about to pull away from the curb when the door to the small house opened, and Anne Prentice came running out.

"Wait! Wait!" they heard her cry. "Please wait! Tell me what I have to sign."

Marta heard her name as soon as she entered the house. She'd finally gone back to the clinic, and she'd had a good long day. It had been busy, and she'd been able to keep her mind off Dominic. It had been good to be away from him. She wheeled herself to the elevator and punched the button. As the lift brought her down the stairs, she could see that the door to her room was open.

"Marta?" Dominic called as the lift shut off.

She rolled over to her room and went in. Dominic was sitting up in bed, waiting for her. There was a video camera mounted on a tripod next to him.

"What's that for?" Marta asked.

Dominic handed her a videotape.

"I made this for you," he said softly.

Marta's hand began to tremble. "What is it?" she asked, suddenly afraid.

"I didn't know what else to do," he said. "I love you."

"Dominic?" Marta asked. "What is this?"

"It's my confession," he said, and the word rang loudly in her ears. She dropped the tape into her lap.

"My confession to the shooting," he continued. "The shooting that crippled you. But not just for that. It's everything. Every crime I ever committed back then. You might think some of them are even worse than what I did to you."

"Worse?" Marta's voice was a whisper of disbelief.

"It's all there," Dominic said, nodding at the tape. "Enough to put me in jail for years."

"Jail," Marta echoed.

"If you decide that's what you want, what you need from me, then I'll go willingly. It's your decision, Marta," he said, his eyes black and beseeching. "The decision to punish or forgive. It's yours alone."

EIGHTEEN

"Here you are," Connor said, leading his parents to their gate at the airport. "I'm sorry that you couldn't stay."

"Tell that person if he's really sorry," Mr. Riordan said to his wife, "he'll go see a priest. Or a doctor."

"Connor." Mrs. Riordan turned to him sadly.

"I heard him, Mum," Connor said, shaking his head.

"Listen, dear, I'm trying to understand—"

"Mum, stop it!" Connor cried. "Please. No more. If you don't believe me, please stop talking about it."

"Connor?" a voice said from behind him. "Aren't you going to introduce me to my in-laws?"

Connor whirled around to find Chelsea beaming at him shyly.

"Unless you want them to keep thinking—"

Connor grabbed her and swung her into his arms. He quieted her with a kiss.

"Connor!" Mrs. Riordan yelped, looking embarrassingly around the airport.

"What the—" Mr. Riordan said.

"Mum, Dad," Connor said happily, holding Chelsea tightly to his side. "*This* is Chelsea. My wife."

"Your—"

"—wife?" Mr. Riordan finished, breaking into a grin.

"I'm sorry I couldn't meet you earlier." Chelsea blushed. "I hope that Connor explained to you. We were . . . having some trouble . . . and . . . I'm sorry," she finished. "But they're personal problems, and we hope to work them out."

"That man in your apartment—" Mrs. Riordan began.

"I told you he wasn't what you thought he was," Connor said.

"But . . ." Mrs. Riordan stumbled, "but . . . she's . . ."

"She's what?" Mr. Riordan asked. "She's a woman. That's what matters." He stepped forward and took off his hat. "Pleased to meet you, Chelsea," he said formally.

Chelsea put out her hand, and Mr. Riordan

ignored it, reaching out and pulling her toward him for a hug instead.

"She's a fine woman, Connor, my boy," Mr. Riordan said happily as he released her.

"Mrs. Riordan?" Chelsea said tentatively, extending her hand.

"Oh, dear," Mrs. Riordan sighed. "I'm so confused."

Connor laughed. "Now you know how I felt."

"I am happy to meet you, Chelsea," Mrs. Riordan said, taking Chelsea's hand in hers. "I'm sorry for what I said."

"It's okay," Chelsea replied reassuringly. "My parents went through the same thing."

"Your parents?" Mrs. Riordan said, with sudden realization.

"Oh, yes," Connor crowed. "Chelsea has a mum and a da. They're black too."

"Connor," Chelsea cried, punching him in the arm. "Don't be mean. Give them a break, will you?"

"I'm sure they're fine people," Mr. Riordan said. "They've raised a fine *daughter,* and that's all that counts."

"Maybe next time, we'll actually spend some time together," Chelsea said.

"Next time, you two can come visit us." Mrs. Riordan suggested with a smile. "It's much . . . quieter there."

The announcement was made for their flight, and Connor's parents went to the gate. They turned and waved one last time, Mrs. Riordan still looking confused, and Mr. Riordan beaming like a lighthouse.

"I love you, Chelsea," Connor said, pulling her into his arms. "Thanks for coming," he whispered in her ear.

Kate and Roan were sitting on the deck off the living room. Roan was wearing a pair of shorts and a halter top. Kate was still in her lifeguarding gear. The sun was high, just disappearing over the house toward the bay. It was late afternoon, and Kate had been in a daze all day. Since she'd watched Justin's plane leave the day before, actually.

She hadn't slept at all last night. She was exhausted and depressed, and she was staring at the ocean in a kind of trance. Out there a woman lay on a raft, drifting away on the waves. Under other circumstances, Kate would have watched with concern. Right now, though, she was imagining being there herself. Out on the waves. In the middle of the ocean. The lulling motion rocking her to sleep. Maybe not on a raft, Kate thought. Maybe on a boat. With Justin.

"Why did you and Justin break up?" Roan

asked suddenly, startling Kate from her thoughts.

"What?" Kate asked, her head flying up.

"I'm sorry," Roan said quickly. "If you don't want to talk about it—"

"No. I'm sorry for snapping at you," Kate said. "I'm just in a lousy mood. And Justin's probably the one person it's hardest for me to talk about right now."

"Are you bummed that he left?" Roan asked hesitantly.

"Bummed?" Kate laughed. "I'm beyond bummed, I guess."

"Why did you break up, then?" Roan asked. "Grace said you're the most normal woman she knows when it comes to men. So what happened? Everyone says you guys got along great."

"It sounds like you're digging for advice," Kate surmised. "Are you worried about something?"

Roan shrugged. "I just want to understand more."

"About relationships?"

"How to make them work. I don't want to make any more mistakes," Roan admitted. "I really don't know much about having a boyfriend."

"I don't know if I can help. Did Grace really say I was normal?" Kate sighed. "I guess I am practical. One thing I've learned, Roan, is not to try and think things out too much."

"What do you mean?"

"Well, here you are, asking me for advice. You've already asked other people, too. You think that if you get all of the information you need, it will somehow be easier to figure things out. But if you want the truth, that was why Justin and I broke up." Kate looked out at the woman on the raft again. It was dangerous, what she was doing, letting herself drift aimlessly in the ocean. It was a risk. The kind of risk Kate had never dared to take.

"It never had anything to do with whether we got along, or whether we liked each other. We still love each other. But I made too many decisions with my head," Kate admitted. "I thought too much about what I wanted. How I wanted it. When and why I should get it. After all that thinking, there wasn't much room left for my heart." Kate sat up and leaned against the railing.

"Sometimes knowing the answers isn't the answer," she said.

"So if you're sorry he left, why didn't you go with him? Didn't he invite you?" Roan asked.

Kate smiled. "Well, he sort of invited me. But he knew I'd say no."

"Why?"

"It's a story that could fill a few books, Roan. Believe me, I asked myself that question a hundred times." Kate looked out at the water, her eyes misting over. "I have to go to college," she said sadly. "I can't just give that up."

"But college doesn't start until September, right?" Roan asked. "You still have the whole summer."

"But now he's gone," Kate said, closing her eyes.

"So?" Roan pressed. "Don't you know where he is?"

Kate was silent for a long time. *You do know where he is,* a voice said in her head. Suddenly Kate's eyes flew open, and they locked on the woman drifting on the ocean waves. *It's a risk,* the voice said, *to drift like that. Sure, it's a risk. And it's about time you took one.*

When Kate turned to Roan, her eyes were shining.

"Thanks for the advice," Kate said, standing.

"The advice?" Roan asked.

"You don't need to talk to anyone, Roan," Kate said, squeezing her shoulder as she passed. "You know what's important already."

"I do?"

Grace pushed open the door and saw Roan out on the deck of the house.

"Hey!" Grace called. "What's up? We're home. Don't you want to hear about our trip?"

David closed the door behind her and grabbed her tightly.

"I love you," he said. "Now calm down, or

you're going to scare the hell out of her, Mother Hen!"

Grace laughed as Roan came toward them across the living room.

"I've got a proposition for you," Grace said, her eyes dancing.

"What?" Roan asked.

"If you want," Grace said slowly. "If you want, you can stay here. With me. For real."

"Stay?" Roan said, her eyes wide. "What do you mean, for real?"

"I mean for good." Grace laughed. "Legally. No runaway status. No Family Services. Roan," Grace said, putting her hand on the girl's shoulder. "I spoke with your mother yesterday."

"My mother?" Roan gasped. "You saw her?"

"She's a beautiful lady," David said. "You look a lot like her."

"She is? I do?" Roan stumbled. "How is she?"

"She's good," Grace said.

"And . . . and is she . . . alone?" Roan asked hopefully.

Both Grace and David shook their heads.

"But I met her," Grace continued. "And I told her you were with me. I told her that I wanted to help you. She signed this for you, Roan." Grace pulled out the document that gave her legal custody of Roan.

"He didn't want her to," Grace said, knowing

Roan needed to understand that her mother had tried, had done what was right. "But she did it anyway. Because she wants something good for you. She doesn't want you to be running anymore."

Roan took the paper and looked at it closely.

"This means you'll take care of me?" she asked tentatively.

"If you want to stay, I'm your guardian," Grace agreed.

"I want to stay," she said simply, overwhelmed with happiness.

"Then it's settled," Grace said, giving Roan a hug. "Welcome to the family."

"This is weird," Roan said, laughing through her tears.

"Think of me as your big sister," Grace suggested. "But ask Bo before you get too excited. Sometimes having a big sister can really cramp your style. Especially when she gets to give you a curfew." Grace winked. "By law."

"So I heard the news," Bo said, finding Roan out on the patio behind the house. "Grace is your legal guardian? She's mine, too. Did you know that?"

"No, I didn't," Roan admitted. "I thought she was just your sister. I hope it doesn't bother you."

"No." Bo shook his head. "Not if it means you'll be staying here."

"I'm glad."

"But does this mean we're related?" Bo asked in confusion.

"I don't think so," Roan answered. "I mean, we're not. We know we're not."

"I know. But I'm talking law-wise."

Roan shook her head. "Grace isn't adopting me—she's just going to be my guardian."

"Hmmm," Bo muttered, perplexed. "But I'm confused," he admitted. "Does this mean . . . is this going to . . . are things with us going to change?"

"I don't know," Roan admitted. "I don't see why they should."

"Because I can't treat you like a sister, Roan," Bo said vehemently.

Roan smiled and looked away.

"I can't treat you like a brother, Bo," she said quietly.

Bo came over and sat down next to her. He leaned toward her, and touched her cheek with his fingers. He touched his lips to hers once, softly, and sighed. Then he kissed her again, slowly. He leaned back and shook himself.

"You're not my sister," he said. "That's for sure."

"Dominic?" Marta asked, her wheelchair poised in the doorway of her room. "Would you like to watch some TV? There's a great light-weight boxing match on tonight."

Dominic lifted his head and turned to her slowly, his eyes confused. "Boxing?" he asked. "You like boxing?"

Marta shrugged. "Why, don't you?"

Dominic shook his head sadly. "I used to be a big fan," he admitted. "I don't watch it anymore, though."

"Well, okay. There's also a great old black-and-white horror movie."

"Horror?" Dominic asked, starting to smile. "It wouldn't be *Dracula* by any chance, would it?"

"Why," Marta laughed, "are you missing your job?"

"A little," he admitted.

"I miss it too," Marta said.

"You do?" Dominic asked, surprised.

"Yeah," Marta said. "I miss the way you looked with your teeth in."

She could see that Dominic was confused. She was flirting with him, and he didn't know how to take it.

"Come on," she urged. "Come watch with me. Don't you want to see if he looks better in his costume than you did in yours? I do, but I already doubt he can top you."

Marta helped Dominic to the couch and turned on the TV. Then she pulled herself out of her wheelchair and settled down onto the couch next to him. He was sitting stiffly beside her, keeping his hands in his lap.

The movie came on, and Marta grabbed the remote controls. She used one to turn on the VCR.

"This movie isn't on often," she explained to Dominic when he noticed the flashing light, signaling that the VCR was taping the TV, go on.

"It's one of my favorites," she continued. "I'd like to have a copy. But I didn't have an extra tape around."

Marta turned to look at him. His eyes were the deep black of the night sky. "I'm using that tape you gave me," she said. "I hope you didn't need it back for anything important."

"Nothing as important as this." Dominic's voice was a whisper as their lips met.

NINETEEN

Justin was pretty proud of himself. He'd gotten the boat ready for the water in only a week. Of course, he'd worked almost sixteen hours a day. The weather was great, and there wasn't any reason to loiter. Certainly not anyone to stop working for. The island was beautiful, from what he could tell, but he had hardly seen more than the dry dock. He was too eager to get going to spend any time as a tourist.

"Okay, Mooch, are you ready to try this again?" Justin asked his dog. "I know you were pretty upset before. But I promise I'll never leave you on the boat again."

Mooch whimpered.

Justin sighed, and started preparing to cast off. It seemed such an anticlimax now—no one to leave with, and no one seeing him off. Well, he'd had the first-time jollies already. This must be how it felt to be a seasoned traveler.

He got in the boat and released the lines. Just as he was pushing off, though, he heard someone calling his name. He looked up and did a double take. No. It wasn't possible. She was thousands of miles away, sitting in her life-guarding chair, suntan lotion and a good book beside her.

"Justin!" she screamed, running toward him down the dock.

Maybe he was dreaming, Justin thought. He'd spent so many hours in the sun this past week.

"Justin, wait!"

This definitely wasn't happening.

The bag she threw hit him squarely in the chest and almost knocked him over. He quickly set it down and turned back to see her coming at him in midair.

"Oh, I'm so glad I made it in time," Kate said as she leapt from the dock and landed on the boat. She slid and almost fell, and Justin reached out to grab her. Her golden hair shone in the sun. Her face was tanned and beautiful, and her eyes were radiant.

"If I'd come all this way," she panted, "and missed you, I'd have killed myself."

"If you'd missed me?" Justin said, still hardly believing that she was really with him, that he was holding her. "Are you kidding?" he cried. "We're meant for each other, Kate. Can't you see that yet?"

"I think I can," she said, smiling. "But you still have to promise to get me to school by September," she warned.

"I promise to get you back," he agreed. "But I don't promise that you'll still want to go."

"You've got a few months now to make good on another promise you made to me once," Kate said.

"What promise was that?"

"You promised if I came with you, it would be the best education that I could get."

"Well, don't you think you've learned anything yet?"

"I have," Kate admitted. "I've learned a lot about myself. And about love."

"What better subject could you choose to major in?" Justin smiled.

"Will this trip teach me that, too?" Kate teased, grinning wickedly.

"I still have a few lessons in my bag," Justin said.

"I can't wait to learn them."

"Before we go," Justin sighed, "you'll have to learn a little more about sailing, though."

He laughed, and looked over his shoulder at a whimpering Mooch.

"And the first thing is called Doggie Patrol."

"Justin," Kate growled.

"Okay," he said, lowering his mouth to hers. "That'll be the second thing."